COLTON'S CONVENIENT BRIDE

Jennifer Morey

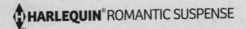

HARLEQUIN® ROMANTIC SUSPENSE

Special thanks and acknowledgment are given to Jennifer Morey for her contribution to The Coltons of Roaring Springs miniseries.

ISBN-13: 978-1-335-66189-0

Colton's Convenient Bride

Recycling programs for this product may not exist in your area.

Copyright © 2019 by Harlequin Books S.A.

HARLEQUIN®

www.Harlequin.com

Printed in U.S.A.

Two-time RITA® Award nominee and Golden Quill award winner **Jennifer Morey** writes single-title contemporary romance and page-turning romantic suspense. She has a geology degree and has managed export programs in compliance with the International Traffic in Arms Regulations (ITAR) for the aerospace industry. She lives at the foot of the Rocky Mountains in Denver, Colorado, and loves to hear from readers through her website, jennifermorey.com, or Facebook.

Visit Jennifer's Author Profile page at Harlequin.com, or jennifermorey.com, for more titles.

To Maddie, who always had her inner wolf.

Chapter 1

In his jeans and nothing else, Decker Colton sprinkled sugar over his grapefruit, trying to think of a way to gently tell Cynthia they weren't working out as a couple.

He'd dated her for three months now and had begun to get the sense that she felt more for him than he for her. Decker found her online—that's how he met all the women he dated. He had no time to search the traditional way and never mixed romance with work. She'd also begun to stay the night too often over the last month and demand more of his time. All this closeness was beginning to feel suffocating. He needed to be free again.

She looked up from her butterless toast and smiled seductively.

With his stomach recoiling, he walked over to the brown, black and cream-colored granite-topped kitchen island where she sat and took the seat next to her. Putting down his bowl of a half grapefruit, he started to scoop the fruit out for a bite.

"I've been thinking," Cynthia said.

Oh no, here it came.

She put her hand over his forearm. "We've been hitting it off really well these last few weeks."

"Cynthia…"

"We should move in together. Whether here or the suite you have at The Lodge."

He swallowed and almost choked on grapefruit juice. After clearing his throat, he saw her wary gaze. Now or never.

He put down his spoon. "Actually, I've been meaning to talk to you."

"You feel the same, don't you?" Her insecurity showed.

"No. I'm sorry… I don't. I don't want to hurt you, Cynthia, but I haven't been comfortable with you staying here as much as you have. We've only known each other a few months."

"But…we've been sleeping together."

"Yes, and that part is great," he said quietly. "However, I'm just not ready for a committed relationship right now." Not with her, anyway.

"You do work a lot. I understand that. I wouldn't stop you from doing what you love. In fact, that's something I love about you, Decker."

She probably loved his wealth.

"It's over, Cynthia." He'd already warned her he wasn't interested in anything lasting. She must not have believed him.

"Over?" She drew back with an indrawn breath. "But…"

"I'm sorry. Really." He honestly did not intend on hurting her but he could see she was quite hurt. He couldn't figure out if losing a man with money hurt more than losing him as a man.

"If you didn't feel the same, then why did you sleep with me?"

"You came to my suite when I didn't invite you. You also showed up here at my house and stayed the night when I didn't ask you to."

She flattened her hand on the counter. "Well, that's insensitive of you."

How was that insensitive? She'd made presumptions and come over uninvited.

"You led me on."

He shook his head. "No, I was honest with you from the start."

"You made me believe you wanted to be with me. All those nights…"

"I did want to be with you. I just don't feel enough for you to keep seeing you."

Standing, she took her purse which she'd hung on the back of the stool and slung it over her shoulder. Then she stood there looking at him, lips pursed and eyes fiery. Then the anger began to ease and she simply regarded him as though seeing him for the first time.

"You really don't believe in love, do you?"

Decker sighed. He'd told her as much when they'd first met, so he said nothing. It wasn't that he didn't *believe in love*. Some people did find it in their lifetime.

But true love was a precious rarity, and with his busy work schedule and fierce ambition, he had little time to date. That only reduced his already slim odds of finding that kind of love.

Cynthia scoffed. "That makes you a waste of time."

With that she turned and walked out of the kitchen.

Decker stood and followed her to the front door, which she flung open and then stepped out into heavily falling snow like a regal, rejected princess.

He might deserve her parting comment, but he also couldn't help the way he felt. He definitely did not enjoy hurting women. Maybe it was time to take a break from them. The Lodge kept him busy and he had plans to make improvements. At this stage of his life, that took priority.

Reaching the doorway, Decker saw his dad get out of his Range Rover, then look over at Cynthia as she marched through the snow and climbed into her own car. She didn't wait for the engine to warm, just turned on the windshield wipers and drove the circle driveway to the long road that led to the highway.

He lived close to The Lodge, on the same property but secluded enough for privacy. He'd built his house, a big log home that was far too spacious for just him, on a mountainside with a view of the Colorado Rockies. He could see the peak of Mount Evans from his upper deck.

Russ Colton walked inside. "She wasn't worthy of you anyway, son."

"I broke up with her this morning."

"From the looks of it I thought maybe she left you." His dad took off his jacket and hung it above the bench in the entry. Sixty-five and CEO of The Colton Empire, as he liked to call it, Russ was tall like his sons but getting thick in the middle. He had graying dark hair, and dark eyes. He prided himself on building the family company—The Colton Empire—which was comprised of the elite and sprawling ski lodge and resort and The Chateau down in the valley.

"I wish she would have," Decker said.

"She was too soft. Too weak. You need a partner who can stand by you as your equal."

Cynthia had clung a little too tightly. He supposed that's what had turned him off and made their relationship feel wrong.

"You need someone like that Hadley woman."

He'd heard Kendall had returned to Roaring Springs a couple of years ago. He hadn't seen her yet, hadn't seen her since high school. Kendall had been one of those kids who'd had her circle of friends and steered clear of the popular crowd. She hadn't participated in sports. He remembered her as the bookish type, which he'd admired since he had liked and excelled in academia. What had always fascinated him was how a girl as pretty as Kendall could have escaped being popular. Now that he was older he knew it had been a choice.

"What's she doing back in Roaring Springs?" he asked curiously.

"Working for her father at Hadley Forestry. From what I hear she's a great asset. She's their conservation consultant."

What did a conservation consultant do? Decker didn't know much about logging and milling or forest management.

"She's working on preserving species of animals in the forested areas they own," Russ supplied. "Got her masters in wildlife biology from Colorado State University. Four-point-o."

"How do you know all that?"

"I ran into her father a few weeks ago. He did some bragging."

Ahh. And, apparently, that's what got his father thinking.

"Now that you're single again," his father went on, "I'd like to talk to you about something I've had rolling around in my head the last few weeks."

Decker followed Russ from the entry to the great room, where the ceiling rose to exposed beams and a gabled window offered a stunning view of the forest and mountain peaks. The kitchen was open to this room, with a long, six-seater island and plenty of white cabinets. The dining area was in a turreted space off the kitchen, something he never used.

His father crossed behind a sofa with a console table running along the back. The sofa faced a stone block fireplace, flanked by two chairs. A big square coffee table had books about exotic places to travel and a decorative ceramic bowl with stone balls inside that matched the earthy color theme of the room.

Russ stopped before the windows and after a few seconds, turned. "Bernard and Marion Hadley have lived on a neighboring ranch for nearly as long as we've been here running this resort."

"Yeah, they have." Decker couldn't begin to guess

where his father was headed with this. Surely he wouldn't suggest he and Decker take on forest management.

"Bernard's been successful. He's made millions running that company."

Russ did respect people who made successes of their lives. He'd raised Decker to do the same. But why single out the Hadleys?

"How did you meet the woman who just left, Decker?" his dad asked.

"Online."

"That doesn't seem to be working for you."

"Not with her," Decker said.

"What would you think about reconnecting with Kendall?"

He hadn't even thought about reconnecting with her, least of all as a love interest. "I think I need a break from women. Cynthia took up too much of my time, and I need to concentrate on The Lodge."

"You do well multitasking, son. What I have in mind is actually related to business. If two families as affluent as the Hadleys and the Coltons joined forces, The Colton Empire would become even greater than it is." Clearing his throat, he pinned Decker with a hard stare. "We have to think of our future and the future of family yet to come. We're doing well now, but I want to plan for the next century or two, maybe more. As long as I'm breathing I won't stop working to increase Colton wealth. It's security."

Decker couldn't disagree there. His father had noble intentions. He wasn't fooled, however. His father's main interest was money.

"You want to arrange for Kendall and me to become romantically involved?"

Russ stepped closer, his serious face warning Decker to brace for impact. "I'd like to suggest more than that. I'd like you to consider marrying her."

"Marrying…" Flummoxed, Decker had to assemble his thoughts. "You want me to *marry* her?"

"You said it yourself, Cynthia took too much time away from you. And you've had to resort to online dating because you don't have time to find a woman who will be able to put up with your work schedule. You're getting older. Don't you want children?"

"Yes." He did want that. He also wanted a family. Wife. Kids. A full house to come home to after a long day at work. His dad was right but what he suggested seemed radical.

An *arranged marriage*?

"Kendall has her own career. She's an only child. When her parents go, she'll be the sole beneficiary."

There his dad went again on his drive for wealth and prosperity. "She'll never agree to it." What smart woman would? Kendall could have anyone. Why would she agree to an arranged marriage…with him?

"Have you spoken with her?"

"No. But when I ran into her father, we talked a while. He mentioned you and Kendall knew each other from high school and made a comment that the two of you would make a fine couple. He said he always wondered why you never hooked up in high school."

Kendall had been a year behind him in school. Her standoffish nature had deterred him from considering

asking her to prom or even out on a date. She hadn't
been standoffish in a snobby way. She had been more
untouchable, as though she had not wanted anything to
do with certain crowds of people. She had seemed more
interested in learning and her own circle of friends. He
didn't even know if she ever dated anyone in high school.

"You're thirty-four, son. You should start a family
soon. Don't wait too long."

Was he crazy for actually considering what his father
proposed? He turned and walked toward the kitchen,
rubbing his chin in agitation. Was he about to do as his
father asked as he always had? Or had Russ Colton just
come up with the perfect solution?

Kendall arrived back home well after dark. She'd
spent the day observing a small pack of gray wolves.
The sighting had been a rare treat. These wolves were
endangered and most sightings had been unconfirmed.
She had learned of one kill north of Kremmling where a
man thought he killed a coyote but it was a gray. She'd
be busy working on protecting them. If they wandered
too far, there would be no telling what ranchers fearing
for their livestock would do.

Wearily she removed her coat and boots and then
went to get ready for a shower. Removing the tie from
her long blond hair, she heard the doorbell rang.

Who would stop by at this hour? Her parents were
usually in for the night by seven, and it was nearly eight.
She was hungry and longing for a bath.

Peeking out the window, she saw her dad. She
opened the door with a questioning look.

"Sorry. Where were you all day?" He entered and shook off snow that had spotted his outerwear. He must have walked from the house.

"It's my day off. I went for a hike." She shut the door as he removed his jacket and hat. "I spotted a small pack of gray wolves. They were so beautiful and they look pretty healthy."

"Huh."

Her father's aloofness when it came to the environment sometimes annoyed her. "I reported their location to the Parks and Wildlife service. They're going to try to tag one."

"I need to talk to you about something important."

"Dad," she complained.

"Gray wolves. Yes. That's wonderful, honey."

"They're an endangered species. Do you know how significant it is that there's a pack in Colorado?" She'd seen only four but that was probably more than anyone had ever seen in several decades.

"That's wonderful, honey." He leaned over and kissed her cheek. "I know how much you love nature."

She forgave him his indifference—as always. "What's up?"

Kendall went into her kitchen. She lived in a house she had built on her parents' property. It was large for one person. A four-bedroom stone Tudor, it had steep rooflines and lots of white-framed windows.

"You'll never guess who stopped by earlier today."

She took out the ham salad she'd made last night and began preparing a sandwich. "Who?"

"Russ Colton." Her dad took a stool at her two-seat island.

Russ Colton? As in, Decker Colton's dad?

"Do you want anything?" she asked, reaching for a bottle of water in the fridge.

"No thanks. Your mom and I had dinner and tea afterward."

She cracked open a bottle and took a drink.

"Russ and I got to talking about you and Decker."

Gosh. She hadn't seen Decker in years. She'd thought about him when she'd first arrived home, wondering if he'd changed. She'd had a crush on him in high school, not that he ever noticed. He'd been insanely popular and very active in school programs. Smart and ambitious too. Tall and well built, he had thick, black hair that would probably never recede and dark eyes that held an intensity that had magnetized her. All the girls wanted him, though, and that had shied her away.

"He's running The Lodge now, isn't he?" She already knew he was. Decker had always sparked her interest and curiosity. She felt that same unruly excitement she had when she was in high school, as though knowing he was out of her league made him all the more desirable.

"Yes, and Russ talked about him someday taking over the entire operation."

Decker stood to inherit a fortune, then.

"Russ said he asked Decker if he'd be interested in partnering up with you and he is."

Partnering up? She set the bottle down and searched her dad's face. He seemed hesitant to say what he obviously worked his way toward.

"You mean a business relationship?"

"In a way. Decker is a busy man. He doesn't have a lot of time to spend building a relationship with a woman."

"Whoa." She held up her hands. "Relationship? What are you getting at, Dad?"

"The Hadleys and the Coltons would make a powerful partnership. Decker wants a family. You're devoted to your work. You'd make him a fine wife, honey. He'd be lucky to end up with someone like you."

She dropped her mouth open. Was he suggesting what she thought?

"You want me to marry him?"

"Russ and I thought the two of you could get together and see if it's a viable possibility."

"But…you want this to advance your business." Anger began to simmer up. Her own father had used her as a pawn, an asset to tempt the mighty Russ Colton.

"This wasn't my idea, Kendall. Russ is the one who brought it up."

"But you eagerly agreed to put up your own daughter as collateral."

"No. It isn't like that. I wouldn't have agreed to anything if I didn't think you and Decker would make a good pair. You liked him in high school."

"I did not," she replied abruptly.

"Your mother told me. You mentioned him a couple of times and she caught you looking at his picture in your yearbook."

Kendall didn't recall talking about Decker, but maybe she had asked a few questions, as intrigued as she had been by him. "What does Mom think about this…arrangement?"

"She doesn't like it."

"But you came here anyway?"

"I talked her into it," he replied in a low, even tone. "I promised I wouldn't make you do anything you didn't want to do."

She wouldn't let him anyway. Her mother probably knew that and it was the only reason she let him come and talk to her.

Kendall considered her father a while. He loved her; she had no doubt about that. But he too often used her as leverage to advance the company. This had to be the worst he'd ever done—agreeing to try to marry her off to a stranger.

Well, Decker wasn't a complete stranger, but she didn't really know him.

"I'll think about it," she said. She just wanted to be alone.

"Russ invited us over for dinner tomorrow night."

Shock jolted through her. He had made dinner plans without talking to her first? Why? Did her father plan on reintroducing them? Did he hope they'd be attracted? More likely he hoped her teenage crush would reignite.

"You're making me feel used," she said tightly.

He put his hand over hers and gave her a squeeze. "I would never do that, honey. You're my daughter. You're the most important thing in my life."

Yeah, and sometimes the most valuable asset.

Though she'd never admit it to her dad, the notion of seeing Decker again did rather intrigue her. She wasn't

the shy girl in high school anymore. And from all she'd
heard about Decker, The Lodge was his one and only
true love. She wondered how a company could steal a
man's heart that way. Didn't he want to find happiness
with a woman? Have a family? And if not, why? Curiosity got the better of her then.

"All right." She'd like to see for herself how Decker
Colton had turned out. Just because she had dinner with
him didn't mean she'd marry him to save her family's
business, however.

Her dad smiled, more from relief than excitement
over having dinner with the pompous Russ and Mara
Colton. At least, Kendall had always considered them
that way. Maybe she had listened to talk around town,
that Russ and Marion held themselves far above the
less fortunate.

After her father left, Kendall skipped her bath and
spent the next thirty minutes searching for her high
school yearbooks. She found them in the basement in
a box with other items she had held dear in those days.
Taking the whole thing upstairs to her bedroom, she
turned on a family movie channel and began spreading
out a journal and other items she had saved for future
reminiscence. Ticket stubs to amusement parks, museums, concerts and movies brought back a lot of fond
memories. She had planned to put them into a scrap-
book but hadn't gotten around to it. She had also kept
little trinkets her friends had given her over the years.
She still stayed in touch with the four women who had
been her closest friends since the seventh grade. Picking up some colorful wristbands, she smiled with the

memory. They had all decided to exchange wristbands for Easter and these four were the ones she'd received.

She'd kept a close-knit group of friends all through school. She hadn't been into cliques and hadn't understood the importance placed on popularity. Life was so much bigger than that. She'd gone into forestry because she loved nature. She also loved the alone time.

Maybe being an only child had made her somewhat of a loner. Never much for social gatherings, she'd preferred to spend her time reading novels and bird-watching.

Setting the wristbands aside, her curiosity nudged her to move on to the yearbooks. "Well, Mr. Colton," she said, "let's have a recap and then see how you turned out."

She opened her sophomore yearbook and passed over some of the notes signed on the pages until she reached a page with Decker standing up as class president. He was a junior that year. She flipped to the page containing his photograph and stared. She wondered if he still had those boyish dark good looks. He'd been tall and lean. Maybe he'd filled out some more since then. She remembered passing him in the halls every once in a while. Sometimes he noticed her. She could still feel the jolt of excitement over the way his eyes connected with hers. Had she imagined his interest? Back then she'd fantasized about going to the prom with him, making all the girls envious. It seemed so silly now.

She moved on to her junior yearbook. Brushing photos and other memorabilia aside, she rolled onto her stomach, lifted her calves and wiggled her toes as she drew the book front and center.

There were several pictures of him that year. How

many times had she turned to them just to look at his cute face?

As the warm, familiar tingles of attraction enveloped, her phone rang.

Abandoning her comfy pose, she scooted to her side and stretched for the phone. "Hi, Mom."

"How did it go?"

"As usual."

"Moving the company forward?"

Kendall loved her mother's understated wit. "Yes." She lay on her back and stared at the ceiling. Not much to look at but she didn't need a painting. She still saw Decker's face.

"He didn't offer you up like some fourteenth-century daughter of a king, did he?"

"No. He gave me the option of meeting him first."

Her mother laughed, a deep, genuine sound that filled Kendall with a surge of love. Then she quieted and sobered. "Sweetheart—"

"Don't, Mom." Kendall knew what her mother would say.

"What if you enter into this and he…"

"Only wants me for the business deal?"

Her mom let out a short, tense breath. "Yes." Then she perked right back up to the pistol Kendall had grown up with. "I've been going over and over how Decker would respond to his greedy father telling him he had to marry you and I'm just…worried."

"Don't be."

"Well, what if he would do it just to please his father?"

Kendall had been away at college and worked another job before coming home at her father's request. She didn't know much about Decker, the man he'd become.

"Maybe he's not like his father. He's successful. That might be their only similarity."

"You always were an optimist. But why would you go through with it? Even the dinner?" her mother asked, sounding concerned.

"I'm…" She wasn't sure how honest she wanted to be right now. "Curious." That was honest.

"Satisfying a high school crush?" her mother asked.

"Yes." And maybe secretly linking in with her young heart, wondering if they'd work out and if it would be as great as she imagined.

"Please be careful, sweetie. If he's half as much of a shark as his father, he's incapable of loving anyone."

She felt a moment of doubt. Maybe dinner was a foolish idea. She could argue she was doing this for her father, but that wasn't entirely true. Then again, how would she ever know if Decker was worthy of her— even in an arranged marriage—if she didn't at least see him face to face?

"I'll know after the dinner."

"I wonder if he's still as good-looking," her mother mused.

"That would be a bonus," Kendall quipped.

"Or a problem."

Chapter 2

Decker stood in the living room of the Colton Manor where his parents resided. A thirty-five-million-dollar, eighteen-thousand-square-foot mansion above the valley, it had seven bedrooms, eleven bathrooms, a wine cellar, an indoor pool and much, much more. Saying the place was nice didn't do it justice, but this kind of excess wasn't to Decker's taste. Decorated quite modern, nothing personal filled the luxurious space.

He waited before the wall of windows with a view of a portion of the gondola that started at The Chateau in the valley and ended at The Lodge. Russ and Mara talked behind him on the sofa. They had an amenable but businesslike relationship in his opinion. Sometimes he wondered if they ever truly loved each other. They both worked all the time. This rare display of them conversing like a couple felt odd.

The front doorbell rang. Kendall and her parents had arrived.

He rarely got nervous but a flash of anxiousness arrested him for a moment. After all these years, he'd finally see Kendall again.

Russ and Mara's butler led the Hadleys into the living room. Bernard came first, in a dark suit and tie. Adorned in a tasteful beige-and-black dress, Marion strolled in next beside her daughter. His breath hitching ever so slightly, Decker's gaze drifted over Kendall as she walked in calf-high black boots with the grace of a ballet dancer. The short-sleeved black dress she wore was fitted to her bodice, waist and hips and the sweetheart neckline exposed some cleavage. She'd left her long wavy blond hair down and other than mascara, had applied a soft rosy gloss to her full lips. Her bright blue eyes zeroed in on him.

He could never have anticipated the strength of the punch in seeing her. She'd obviously matured, but oh. What a woman.

He swallowed—an involuntary reaction. Wow.

She seemed to spend a few seconds inspecting him, as well. Those stunning eyes—he didn't remember them being so darn blue—ran up his body, went all over his chest and arms and finally landed on his face. He hadn't worn a suit, just a nice long-sleeved ocean-blue shirt with gray pants and leather loafers. He had chosen a tie.

"Kendall." He stepped forward. "It's so good to see

you again." He took her hand and dipped his head to kiss it, seeing her face up close now. She had a few freckles but they somehow enhanced her beauty.

"Y-you too."

By her stutter and slightly bewildered look, he suspected she hadn't expected to like what she saw as much as she did, which matched his reaction. He caught his father's approving gaze with a subtle, almost shrewd, grin.

Bernard and Marion went to Russ and Mara and started a conversation while a servant appeared with a tray of champagne flutes. Kendall took one and then Decker did also.

"Dad tells me you've been working for Hadley Forestry as a conservancy consultant." Might as well start with the small stuff.

"Yes. I worked for a company in Fort Collins after college but my dad needed me here."

"He needed you?" Decker didn't know much about the forestry industry or her father for that matter.

"He's getting older. He needs help running the company. I think someday he'd like to see me take over."

"Is that what you want?"

She looked away as she thought. "I do love my degree and my work. Running Hadley Forestry would be right in line with that. I'm just not sure I want that level of executive responsibility. I'm an outdoor girl."

"You could always hire a CEO."

She smiled. "I've thought of that. My dad isn't crazy about someone outside the family running his baby."

Decker nodded with a grin. "My dad wouldn't care. He'd only care that his baby made lots of money."

She stopped smiling as she turned to look over at Russ as though a rumor or two had just been confirmed.

"Don't worry," Decker said, trying to keep things light—and hopefully putting her at ease. "I'm nothing like him."

That pretty smile returned, as did her gaze. "Good to know."

"At the risk of seeming ignorant, what, exactly, does a forestry company do, aside from chopping down trees and selling lumber?"

"There is a supply side and a conservation side," she explained. "We do a lot of logging, milling and forestry management. We supply Douglas fir, western larch, ponderosa pine and lodgepole pine to the building industry and since I've started, we're looking into partnering with the World Wildlife Fund." She released a breath before continuing. "Also, one of the first things I did when I came on was to arrange for the company to start harvesting trees destroyed by mountain beetle. It's proven to provide a great supply source for the company and clears out forested land."

"Impressive."

"Conservation is my specialty." She smiled, revealing straight white teeth. "What about you? You run The Lodge? It's a lot bigger than when I left for college."

"Yes. The original ski lodge is now staff housing. The new lodge is much larger and glamorous. There are restaurants and, of course, hotel rooms."

"Luxury hotel rooms?"

"Yes. We also built some cabins on the property."

"Luxury."

Did she not approve? "We do cater to the wealthy. You grew up that way, didn't you?"

"Yes. My family is very wealthy. I just think average people should be able to enjoy places like The Lodge."

"They can," he countered. "The ski resort is open to everyone."

"They just can't stay the night there."

She clearly didn't like the segregation of classes. He both admired her for that and disagreed. "Some people need places to go to escape the public."

"Then maybe you are more like your father than you think."

"Do you not like my father?"

Again, she glanced over at Russ. "I guess he's not much different than mine."

"Using his kid to advance business?" He grinned.

She smiled back and then laughed softly. "Yes."

After a long look that began to sizzle, she said neutrally, "I haven't been to The Lodge since it was expanded."

"I'll have to take you on a tour sometime." Maybe then she'd change her mind.

"I'd like that."

He barely heard the announcement that dinner was ready, just followed Kendall into the formal dining area, a rectangular room with a polished wood table that could seat fourteen, white fireplace on one side and china cabinet on the other. Swooping curtains adorned tall windows and a crystal chandelier hung from a tray ceiling.

Russ finished bragging about his empire's first quarter projections as he took a seat next to Mara, who appeared bored and didn't say much. Decker sat beside Kendall when she took a seat next to her mother.

"As two of the most affluent families in Roaring Springs, I can't think of a better alliance," Russ said.

Bernard smiled. "I couldn't agree more."

Marion eyed her husband and then glanced across at Mara, who quietly observed her, evidently having noticed that Marion didn't seem happy to be here. Decker's mother valued the time she spent with her children and grandchildren but her devotion to The Chateau made that a challenge.

"I am curious, however," Bernard said. "What made you think Decker and Kendall would make such a good match?"

"You've been getting a lot of good press with your move toward preserving the forest. World Wildlife Fund. Environmental financing. Very innovative revenue generation."

Bernard puffed up in what Decker could only call pride. "That was my daughter's idea."

Decker watched his difficult-to-impress father bestow rarely offered respect upon Kendall and he could almost hear him thinking what a great addition she'd make to his Colton Empire.

"We're ready, sir."

Decker turned to see a servant standing at the entrance to the dining room.

"Ah," Russ said. "Decker, I've taken the initiative to arrange for you and Kendall to have a more private dinner." He chuckled briefly. "You're too old to be having dinner with your parents on a first date. Charles here will take you to your table."

Decker saw Kendal's startled face and didn't make a big deal over his own surprise. They followed the servant to the front side of the mansion, where a sunroom overlooked the picturesque valley. Decker suspected his mother had something to do with the round linen-covered table with a candle burning and soft piano music playing. Two chairs flanked the double French entry and plants lined the stone wall.

Decker pulled out a chair for Kendall and then sat across from her, looking out the arch-topped window beside them.

"This is awkward."

He turned back to Kendall. "Our parents are determined to put us together."

"Hm." She lifted a glass of red wine and sipped. "Not my mother."

"She's against it?"

"She wants to see me marry for love. She only agreed because I wanted to have this dinner with you and decide for myself."

"I'm not sure what my mother thinks," Decker admitted. "She probably agrees with my father. She's just as ambitious as he is when it comes to the success of the business."

"No wonder he came up with this plan. He sounds like my father." Kendall smiled, but it didn't reach her eyes.

"Business first."

"Always. But he does have his redeeming qualities and I do know he loves me."

"I feel the same about my father," Decker said. "He's forgotten how to show love, but it's there. Maybe he never learned how to show it." He sometimes resented that and wondered if the constant fight to win Russ Colton's love had compelled him to do anything his father asked or expected. Sometimes he wished he would have followed his brother's path. Wyatt dropped out of college to join the rodeo. Only when he inherited the Crooked C Ranch from their grandmother did he return to Roaring Springs.

"Well, now that they have us where they want us, what shall we talk about?" she murmured.

He leaned back as a servant delivered the first course. More interested in her, he ignored the artful display of sliced seared scallop topped with alaea red salt and lemon olive oil.

"What have you been up to since high school?" he asked.

"I went to college and got my masters. After that I went to work for the Forest Service. Then I returned to Roaring Springs when my father said he needed me home, to help with the company. He's getting older and, as I mentioned earlier, thinking about retiring."

"Is that all? What about relationships?"

She lifted her brow marginally, as though she hadn't expected the question. "I've had boyfriends. Nothing worth talking about."

"Those are usually the most important to talk about."

"If that's what you think, then tell me about your past girlfriends." She sipped her wine and sent him a coy look with those incredible blue eyes.

Well, he'd stepped right into that one. "Nothing too serious. I thought I loved the girl I was with after high school but then I grew up."

"The prom queen?"

He grunted because it all seemed so meaningless now. "Yeah." Then he contemplated her a moment, such a beautiful woman and she'd never stepped out into the spotlight. "You kept a low profile in high school."

"I was more into real friends."

He had run across a lot of students who had befriended him because of his popularity. It hadn't bothered him, though. He'd had his close group of companions.

"What about after the prom queen?" she asked.

She wouldn't give up. "I dated someone in college."

"All through college?"

"Yes, and then she didn't want to move to Roaring Springs so she broke up with me."

"Did that hurt?"

He'd be lying if he said the breakup didn't. His first love had gone to college for business like he had. He thought they made a great team. She was someone his father approved of and she was pretty. Back then pleasing his dad had been priority number one.

"Yeah, but I graduated and went to work for my dad." It struck him then that maybe part of the reason he had done that was to forget about that woman.

"No more time for love."

He paused at her sarcasm because it felt truer than something to joke about. "What about you? Why haven't you been snatched up by someone?"

"Oh, I was. A few times. I had a couple of year-long

relationships that ended mutually, and then closer to graduation I met someone special and we moved in together. I imagined that was going to be it for me until I came home one day to him in our bed with another woman." She sighed. "I never thought I'd be one of those women who so sorely misread a man. Walking in on your lover with someone else happened to other women and only in the movies."

"Not to you?" He chuckled. "I didn't walk in on one of my girlfriends, but she told me she had been with someone else. That was after college. I was working a lot and I guess she got sick of it." He drank some wine as he remembered how much that had stung. The realization that he'd become his father had been difficult to swallow. That's when he'd begun to think how different his life would be had he not listened to the great Russ Colton. He'd envied his brother Wyatt for defying their father and going off to the rodeo before inheriting the Crooked C.

"I've found that waiting for them to come to me works best, rather than actively looking for it," Kendall confided.

He set down his glass as the servants brought in the next course, which was creamed pea-and-leek soup with croutons.

Decker didn't miss how Kendall appreciated the presentation of the dishes. Although she was no stranger to fine dining, she didn't bask in the elegance for the wrong reason, though. The way she took it all in, smelled the aromas, told Decker she loved the art and the tastes more than the privilege. She hadn't lost her humble nature and took nothing for granted.

Like now, she lifted her spoon and smelled with her eyes closed before sampling the soup. When she finished she looked at him and said, "You know what I love most about dinners like this?"

He felt a shot of warmth as he observed her. "No, what?"

"I don't have many meals like this, but when I do, they're always special because they take time. It's more than good food. It's the entire experience, and the social aspect."

He concurred, especially about the time. His curiosity of her grew and he needed to know more. "Is that why you agreed to this dinner?"

She stopped eating the soup. "No, of course not."

It had to be more than him, or more aptly, their fathers coming to her. "Then why even consider marrying me?"

"Why did you even consider marrying me?" she volleyed back.

"I asked you first."

Smiling, giving him another shot of warmth, she murmured, "I guess I haven't really considered it yet. I wanted to meet you. See how it went."

"And how is it going?"

"I'd say quite well." Still looking at him with a soft smile, she asked, "Are you going to answer the question now?"

Decker wasn't ready to let her off the hook yet. She hadn't exactly answered his question. Why did she skirt it? "So you have no intention of marrying me? Why agree to dinner with me, knowing this is all for the purpose of the two of us getting married?"

She took a moment before responding. "Like I said, I wanted to meet you, meet the man and see how the high school boy turned out. Do I have to definitively say I'll marry you yet?"

"I can give you until after dinner," he half joked.

She smiled again, bigger this time. "What about you? Why did you consider marrying me?"

"I'm not sure I did. I worried that I'd do yet another thing my father expects of me," he said.

Her smile faded and her brow lowered as though confused. "Then why…"

"I was curious, too. I remembered you from high school and I had to see you."

"It was the same for me," she confessed.

After a long stare, she lowered her eyes first and he forced himself to pay attention to the soup. His anticipation of continuing this courtship stimulated him more and more.

Minutes later, two servants returned with fresh plates.

"Sea bass served with celeriac purée, sorrel leaves and smoked sauce," one of them said.

Kendall went about her usual delighted inspection before enjoying the first bite.

"What do you like to do in your spare time?" he asked as they shared the meal.

"I love being outside. I also read a lot. Flower garden. Go out for lunch with friends. Spend time with my parents. What about you?"

He chuckled. "I work a lot."

"Surely you must do something other than that. Don't you ever get outside?"

"I ski when I get the chance," he replied.

"How thrilling."

Her teasing didn't offend him. "I read sometimes."

"Hmm…something in common. What about friends?" she asked, no longer teasing.

"I didn't keep in touch with anyone from school. My friends work for me or frequent The Lodge."

"It sounds like you have a bland life." She sounded as though she pitied him.

"Running The Lodge is not bland. I meet all kinds of interesting people."

Kendall contemplated him and he could all but hear her thinking of the affluent people who came to The Lodge, famous or just wealthy and successful. He liked the challenge of running such an upscale establishment.

"What would you have done if you hadn't followed your father's footsteps?" she queried.

Caught off guard, he had to take a few seconds to think. "I would have still chosen business. Growing up, I was always fascinated with the resort and The Chateau. I used to love to ride the gondola and watch all the people. Then when I was older, I paid attention to how my dad made profits. Even before he started pressuring me to work and learn to take over the business, I was already headed for an MBA. But I'm not sure I'd have chosen my father's business. I think I would have chosen to start my own."

Kendall nodded as she absorbed his response. He really liked her genuine interest. It gave him a shot of heat and made him notice how beautiful she was. He had found her beautiful from the moment he saw her but now it had taken on a new intensity, more sexual. He wanted her every time he saw her.

"Would your dad have fired you if you didn't run the business the way he wanted?" Kendall asked.

"Yes." Russ could be a real hardhat when it came to that. "I want to be CEO. So far he isn't convinced I'm the man for the job."

"I suppose that's a good thing. You wouldn't want that role if it would set you up for failure."

"It won't set me up for failure. I'm the only one who can do it." He wasn't bragging like his father often did. He knew he was good enough for that job.

"Well, you certainly seem to work hard enough. And you're in great shape so you must at least have time to take care of yourself."

"I have a gym in my house and there is one at The Lodge. I also do get a lot of exercise just walking the property."

The salad course arrived and Kendall rubbed her tummy. "I don't want to get too full."

There were more courses to come. "You don't have to eat everything."

She lifted her fork. "And miss all this deliciousness? I don't think so." She ate a bite.

"Tell me about your work," he said. "Why forestry?

Were you another victim of a father's dreams and aspirations?"

She smiled, something she apparently did often.
He noticed her again with more intensity, his reaction
sort of taking him by surprise with its immediacy. She
seemed like a happy, confident woman.

"Yes and no. I always knew I wanted to get into a career that involved the environment. My father encour-
aged me to go to school for forestry. I chose wildlife
biology and took some forestry classes."

"What do you love about what you do?"

She pushed the salad away and leaned her elbows
on the table, blurring his view of her through the candle flame. "Being outside. Preserving the forest and
the wildlife."

Humble indeed. She cared about doing good in this
world. She was driven like him. Smart, too. Decker experienced a jolt of excitement along with his increasing
awareness of her, her sexy shape, her hair, her eyes, everything. He definitely wanted to see her again.

"I found a small pack of gray wolves," she said.
"They haven't existed in the Colorado Rockies since the
nineteen forties. Sightings are increasing, which means
they are likely crossing the state line from Wyoming."

"Fascinating." He didn't mean her sighting. He meant
her.

Kendall hadn't expected to enjoy this dinner as much
as she did, and not just the food and the presentation of
the courses. Decker surprised her. He was so honest,
about his father and his work and himself. Gone were

any traces of Mr. Popular in high school. He'd grown into a real man and truly fit the tall, dark and handsome cliché to the *T*. Decker dressed impeccably but not in an overstated way and she sensed his genuine humility and respect for others. That's where he differed from Russ.

She stood from the table. Having finished the rest of the courses of filet mignon, cheese on a wooden board and a remarkably colorful and tasty dessert, she could literally roll out of the sunroom.

Just outside the room, Decker stopped and faced her. "I'm not ready for this to end. How about I show you my favorite part of this house?"

She could put off meeting her parents, who would surely expect a synopsis on how the dinner went. Besides, she was more than a little curious to see what Decker liked most about his parents' gorgeous and ostentatious home.

"I would love that," she said, arrested by his answering grin and how it made his dark eyes smolder.

He led her upstairs and down a hallway. At the end, there was a doorway. To her right she saw a narrow stairway.

"That's for the staff. It leads to the prep kitchen and their quarters."

Decker opened the door at the end of the hall. It was narrower than the others along the way.

He flipped on the light and Kendall found herself looking up another stairway.

The wooden stairs creaked as she stepped up. The space didn't appear to be cared for regularly. The scratched and light-stained wood needed a polish to stand up to the rest of the grandeur of the house.

At the top, Decker entered what appeared to be an attic, or a space that hadn't been finished. Boxes on one side and furniture on the other gave evidence to that end. There were toys on the floor there, along with an open antique trunk that must be worth a fortune. But everything was dusty.

She glanced at Decker, who seemed to be waiting for her reaction.

She had one. "This is your favorite room?" she asked incredulously.

"It's the one with the most character."

He definitely had a point there. The rest of the manor, except the sunroom where they had dinner, was rather cold. Now she was sure he had chosen that room for this very reason.

She felt her heart flutter with greater interest in the man she had only known from afar.

Wandering farther into the six-hundred or so square foot room, she loved the two dormer windows facing the back of the house and the open ceiling. The space had a rustic and unfinished charm.

"The room was too small according to my mother," Decker said. "It turned into a storage area and the servants took it over. Their kids would come up here and play."

"Every kid should have an attic to play in." Kendall smiled. "As long as it's not haunted."

He chuckled. "The house isn't old enough for that, although I'm sure there are plenty of distant Colton relatives who might have cause to haunt us."

Kendall could not believe how much she enjoyed talking to him. He was so witty and had a lurking sense of humor. As she continued to softly smile, his demeanor changed. He watched her like a man who hadn't just had a several-course meal. He watched her hungrily.

"Why do you like this room so much more than the rest of the house?" she asked again.

His gaze scanned the dusty, disheveled room before finding hers again. "It's honest."

"Honest?" She didn't quite understand.

"I wouldn't trade my success or my money for anything, nor would I live in any other kind of house than the one I own, but this—with all its imperfections—is a reminder that humility is important."

She could relate. She respected the wilderness a little bit like that. She liked nice things, just as he did, but being outdoors and in nature, sharing the land with wild animals, was a much different environment. "Not everything has to be perfect and cost a lot."

"I am going to ask the staff to clean the place up, though." He grinned and once again she found herself rapt with fascination over the transformation and the light in his eyes.

"And I did have more of a motive to bring you here," he continued. "Away from prying eyes, I can put to test something that's got me curious."

Hearing and seeing his playfulness, she went along with him. "Oh yeah? What is that?"

He put his hand on her lower back and pulled her gently toward him, until she was flush against him. "I only know of one way to see if we're compatible."

With her hands on his chest and staring up at his face, she did nothing as he lowered his head and kissed her.

Tingles spread from the point of contact. He kept the touch soft and light but the warmth quickly heated into something more passionate. He pressed slightly harder and moved his mouth as though he meant to take the kiss deeper. Instead, he withdrew, letting out a long breath with his eyes smoldering hotter than before.

Kendall let go her own breath, unexpectedly starved for air. He removed his hand and she stepped back.

"Well, that answers my question," he quipped.

Flustered, she said, "W-we should get back. Our parents are probably waiting for us." Decker walked with her through the mansion toward the formal living room, where a servant informed them coffee would be served. Kendall would venture to guess this was when Russ would want to talk about an arranged marriage.

Sure enough, the four parents chatted there, already sipping coffee.

"Ah, here they are." Russ stood from a sofa that faced an identical one where Kendall's parents sat.

She took a chair next to her mother and Decker sat on the one beside her. A beaming Russ sat back down.

"How did it go?" her mother asked.

Feeling like a teenager after a first kiss again, Kendall replied, "Wonderful." She turned to Mara and Russ. "Please give your chef my compliments."

"He is an outstanding executive chef," Russ said. "He vets our chefs for The Lodge and The Chateau."

"Very nice," Kendall murmured.

"Well?" Russ turned to his son. "When shall we plan the wedding?"

Decker looked at Kendall. "That's up to Kendall."

She felt the blood drain from her head with shock. He already wanted to plan a wedding? She did like Decker, but she felt cornered and uncertain. Would she really jump into something like this just because her father had asked her to? Then again, she had not come to this dinner to satisfy her father; well, maybe a little, but being here had been her own choice. She had not agreed to a marriage, not yet. Although the idea definitely tantalized her, and only because she would be marrying Decker, a man who had always fascinated her.

"I'd like to sleep on it," she said.

"No point in rushing anything," her mother concurred.

"They hit it off," her father said. "I can tell."

How could he tell?

"Just set a date," Russ insisted.

"You can call it off if you change your minds," Bernard added.

Russ sent him a sharp glance. "They won't call it off."

"Dad," Kendall protested.

"Just set a date," Russ insisted. "That's all we ask."

"No harm in setting a date," Marion said.

Kendall had to gape at her mother. She had reservations before tonight. What had happened to change her attitude? Mara smiled at that. "I see no harm in setting a date, either. There's a lot of planning that will need to be done. If you both back out at the last minute, then we cancel everything."

Her logic was something of a marvel. They'd plan an expensive wedding and if Kendall or Decker cancelled, oh well? They had a lot of money to burn but to Kendall that was an enormous waste.

How long would she be stuck here if she didn't agree to something?

"It's traditionally the bride's family who pays for the wedding," she said. "I'm not comfortable with making plans when I'm not certain this is going to work."

Russ waved his hands in front of him. "Don't worry about money. I'll pay for everything."

Mara eyed him in disagreement.

"The worst that will happen is we lose some deposits," Russ said.

"I'll select and pay for my own dress." Kendall couldn't believe she'd just said that. She felt sucked into a surreal situation where everything was happening way too fast.

Russ waved his hands again as if all of this amounted to nothing consequential. "We can talk details later. Just pick a date."

Just pick a date.

"March thirty-first," Decker said.

She gaped at him. That was the end of the month, little more than three weeks away. "Are you—"

"Fabulous," Russ exclaimed.

"Wonderful," her father said.

"This should be interesting," Marion murmured.

And Mara just chuckled softly but wryly.

Chapter 3

The next morning Kendall drove the short distance to her parents' house. Her mother had asked her to accompany her for breakfast. While not the mansion of Russ and Mara's scale, it was still an impressive piece of architecture. Her parents didn't like to feel like they could get lost in their own home, or have so much space that most of it was never used. They liked a homier environment, which this six-bedroom abode offered. White and with lots of grouped, tall and arch-topped windows and a varied roofline, it had a sprawling, modern look.

Kendall entered the foyer, a half-circle room with a grand staircase on one side and a small sitting area with a fireplace on the other. Upstairs were two master suites, Kendall's bedroom that her mother had kept for her, a guest room and a study. The landing at the top of the stairs had another sitting area with views of the mountains through high windows above the open foyer.

She walked through the informal living room—the formal living room was off the dining room next to the kitchen. There were also two guest suites on this level along with another study.

Kendall could see her mother in the kitchen talking cheerily with the cook. They only employed a cook and a housekeeper, not a full servant staff like Russ and Mara. A round table in a turret area could seat six.

Kendall passed an arched double entry to an entertainment room with a wet bar and casual seating. Although she couldn't see them from here, a wall of windows could be opened to allow access to the pool. Her parents had divided it to better control humidity.

"There she is." Her mother came to her and gave her a hug. "I asked Carol to make your favorite."

Kendal's favorite breakfast was a veggie omelet, strawberries and rye toast with a good amount of butter.

"You're awfully chipper this morning." Kendall took a seat next to Marion, enjoying the view of the glassed-in pool and the mountainside beyond. The ground was still covered in snow. Still early March, there would be no real thawing for several weeks.

"I want to hear all about your dinner. You weren't very talkative last night. I thought if I gave you some time to process you'd be more of a fountain."

She had always been very close to her mother and wasn't at all surprised that she'd known Kendall needed time to absorb, especially big moments like the one last night.

"It was lovely."

"You already said that last night."

"Decker is…not what I expected. He's a gentleman and ambitious but not obsessed with wealth." To Kendall, money was a necessity and a lot of it definitely made life easier, but it had a purpose and that wasn't to exploit excesses. Decker had struck her as having the same view. "It was refreshing. He's grown up since high school. He doesn't keep in touch with any of the people he hung around with back then."

Her mother smiled fondly. "You've both grown up. I could tell you really liked him last night, and the way he looked at you." She lifted her eyes up in wonder. "He's very attracted to you."

"I'm attracted to him, too, but it's only the first day."

"Are you going to go through with the wedding?" her mother asked.

"I don't know."

"He doesn't want to lose this opportunity. He wants you, Kendall."

"He doesn't even know me," she protested. "I need more than physical attraction."

"He knows you enough and you know him enough. He's got a solid reputation. The physical attraction is important. The rest will come in time."

Kendall sat back and angled her head, perplexed. "Yesterday you were worried about me marrying Decker."

"That was before I saw the two of you together. I still want you to be sure this is what you want, but I feel better about this arrangement now."

Because she knew Kendall had a crush on Decker in

high school and she had witnessed what Kendall had felt with Decker during the dinner. Undeniable chemistry.

"I will be sure," Kendall finally said. At least, she hoped she would be. Given the flutter of attraction she felt for Decker, even now when he wasn't in sight, she just might be able to take the chance on him.

"I can't wait to go dress shopping," her mother said, full of excitement.

"Mother…!"

"We don't have much time. I thought we could start this afternoon."

"I have to work," Kendall protested.

"Your father told me you could take as much time off as you need this month."

Holy bejesus. What had happened to her mother? She had been bitten by a wedding bug for sure.

"I know you, my dear. When you like something you recognize it right away, and I can tell you *really* like Decker Colton."

She did like Decker. Kendall withdrew from how much. She had felt that and more for her last long-term boyfriend when she had caught him with another woman. He'd broken her heart. She never wanted to feel that way again. Maybe that had more to do with her reason for accepting an arranged marriage—or the possibility of one—than curiosity. Because the truth was, she felt oddly safe entering into this kind of relationship. She'd be the one in control and Decker would never be able to hurt her.

But, on the other hand, what her mother suggested made her wonder if she might be too reckless marrying like this.

"He is different than I remember," she conceded, yet still feeling as though she was trying to convince *herself* that meant he'd be worth the risk. But, honestly, did it really matter if he was different? So he'd grown up. That didn't mean he wouldn't end up hurting her.

"How so?"

"Not… showy, or…"

"Immature?" her mother provided.

Kendall wouldn't talk about the popular crowd that had surrounded him in high school and made him seem so untouchable. Unobtainable.

"Yes, but he's so focused on his business. It's the only reason he agreed to this arranged marriage." She didn't want to be second to a man's profession. Then again, she placed high standards on her own career. She was passionate about saving animals and preserving nature.

"Well, you've been consumed with your work, too, Kendall. Ever since that man you were with toward the end of college, you've been driven that way."

Sometimes she wished her mother didn't know her so well.

"Seems to me you both have your reasons why a marriage like this would work," her mother continued.

She wasn't helping Kendall's internal conflict. She'd basically just given her a green light to follow her heart and her heart wanted the excitement of marrying a man like Decker, to see where it would lead.

"Come on," her mother said, "Let's go shopping."

Decker wanted Kendall. He sat at his desk in his large modern office with a seating area before a gas fireplace and a conference table, staring at his computer but thinking of nothing but her.

For once he wanted something for himself and not for his father. Yes, this had been his father's idea, but last night's dinner had changed everything. Kendall was perfect for him. She'd fit his lifestyle better than any other woman he'd met. He'd never been more certain this early on in the relationship game. That served as a reminder that maybe he should tread more carefully. He couldn't afford anything getting in the way of taking over the company.

Kendall didn't appreciate her father using her as leverage. She was smart and didn't have to settle for less than she deserved. Maybe an arranged marriage wouldn't be enough for her. He'd have to work hard convincing her this would be a good union, even if they didn't love each other.

As far as Decker was concerned, love was overrated and marriage was more of a financial investment than anything. He didn't celebrate Valentine's Day and he didn't think wedding anniversaries were anything special. So a couple stayed together for x number of years. Who cared? In this modern, fast-paced world, lasting marriages were becoming rarer and rarer. He'd rather celebrate windfalls or career advancements.

Maybe Kendall wouldn't agree. That's why he'd romance her the traditional way to get her to the altar. Like any business deal, he would go after her aggressively.

"Distracted?"

Decker looked up to see his father enter his office. He never knocked. Seeing his shrewd grin, Decker realized his father meant thoughts of Kendall had distracted him. Russ was clearly pleased with the way things were going, the melding of the Coltons and the Hadleys into one powerful unity.

"A little."

"What's your next move?" his father asked, going to one of the seats before the desk and sitting. He propped his ankle on his knee.

"Maybe flowers or dinner out."

"That's mediocre. Kendall is accustomed to riches. You should fly her to Paris for dinner or something equally grandiose."

"I don't think Kendall is that materialistic." She was into nature, not what money could buy.

"How often does a man take her to Paris for dinner?"

Not often he was sure, but that wasn't the way to win her heart. "I'm old enough to manage on my own, Dad."

Russ's smile broadened. "We can't lose this deal. With Hadley money added to ours, we can expand to a level we've never reached before."

That did appeal to Decker, but his dad didn't understand. "I'm the one who had dinner with her last night. Let me handle the courtship."

His dad's smile faded and he nodded. "You've got a good head for business, Decker. I'll trust you to do a good job with this marriage."

A good job. That sounded cold even to Decker. "Kendall won't go through with this marriage unless she feels it's a smart move on her part." He had to plant that warning in his father's head, prepare him for the possibility that Kendall wouldn't marry him after all.

"Draft up a contract so we have her written agreement to marry by the end of the month."

Decker barely smothered a scoff. One dinner with Kendall and he knew she'd never sign a contract to tie the knot.

"Our lawyers can write it so she'll feel comfortable but we'll have assurance that she'll marry you. If she wants to end it afterward, then we'll get something out of it."

Decker began to feel ill over how Russ reduced something personal to a bottom line. "I'll see what I can do."

Russ nodded. "Very good." He placed his hands on his knees. "Any progress on boosting reservations since that woman's murder?"

Decker had been working tirelessly on a strategy to improve revenue, to replace the losses that homicide had caused. He worried he wouldn't be able to turn things around before the film festival this summer. "I've got meetings scheduled to come up with a mitigation plan."

"Good. Let me know how it goes."

"As always."

"Even though Bianca Rouge was one of the most expensive call girls you can buy in Vegas, her untimely demise still tarnishes our reputation," his dad said. "She stayed at The Lodge. Some people aren't comfortable staying here because of that, a murder victim."

A European millionaire had brought the Rouge woman to The Lodge. While he had suffered his own shame in being caught with a prostitute, he had not been the killer. A man named Nolan Sharpe had written a suicide note confessing to the crime.

"I've got a weekly call with Deputy Sheriff Daria Bloom to get status on her investigation," Decker replied.

"That's all good, but I need to see results. If you're going to be CEO, you should be able to handle a PR disaster like this in a timely manner."

Decker felt his ire rise. His father frequently threw veiled threats like that at him.

"Have I ever failed you?" he asked.

"I can think of a few occasions."

Decker met his father's hard eyes dead-on. "No one else can run this lodge better than I can and you know it."

"All I'm saying is I need more convincing before I promote you to CEO."

No, his father just enjoyed his position of power. Decker had to bite his tongue before he told Russ his ego was the only thing that needed convincing.

"I often wonder how much more successful we'd have been had Wyatt done what he was supposed to and joined our business," his father added, further grating Decker's nerves.

"I doubt he'd have made any impact, given he had no desire to be part of this," Decker said, knowing that would irritate his father. "Unlike me."

Russ's face grew stern with displeasure. "I know you respect him for going off to do what he wanted, but a rodeo star is hardly up to this family's standards."

Decker suspected that could be debatable. "He runs the Crooked C Ranch. That's up to your standards."

Decker watched his father catch that he'd said *your* standards.

After a while, Russ's annoyance eased and a new, slightly shrewd grin inched up more on the left side. "That's what I like about you, son. You never back down. That's what makes the difference between a good CEO and a great one. You have to have the balls to run a business like this." Russ stood.

Decker didn't know what to say. His father had actually complimented him.

Kendall indulged her mother and went with her to Roaring Springs's most elite bridal shop, a boutique that offered both top designer labels and custom-made gowns. She had wavering feelings about this outing. Inner excitement clashed with anxiety over whether she should even be looking at wedding dresses when she was not at all sure she would go through with this absurdly concocted idea of an arranged marriage.

Her leather boots tapped on the wood floor as she passed white-trimmed, inlayed arches in the walls on each side, beautiful wedding dresses hanging next to each other. Manikins in the front windows and placed throughout the shop showcased more. Even if Kendall were certain she'd walk down the aisle to meet Decker at the altar, she'd have a difficult time choosing. But one dress across the shop snagged her attention before she could even scan the rest.

Her mother stopped at a dress hanging in one of the left inlayed arches. It had a lace bodice and off-the-shoulder sleeves; its skirt was sheer over silk and the train not overly long. Meanwhile, Kendall went to check out the dress on a manikin that had caught her eye the moment she'd entered. She often found things that way; something struck her fancy and nothing else matched her taste. Shopping went fast when that happened. She began to let her earlier anxiety go and the excitement take over. What girl didn't like wedding dresses?

Sleeveless and dipping just enough to show a modest amount of cleavage, the bodice was made up of stunning silver-white reflective beads of varying sizes and shapes and round white pearls. The pearls ran down each rib of the corset and the beads thinned over the stomach, revealing see-through lace. The beadwork picked up again at the waist and dipped to a V at the lower abdomen. The Cinderella-style skirt had no train, just a puff of tulle.

"That's lovely," her mother said.

Kendall realized she'd fallen into a distracted study of the dress and hadn't noticed Marion appear beside her.

"Yes. Quite."

"Try it on."

A clerk approached, having seen them admiring the gown. "Would you like a dressing room?"

"Yes, she would," Kendall's mother said.

Kendall sent her an unsure look.

"Go, go, go." Her mother shooed her beneath the smiling clerk's eyes.

After the clerk retrieved her size, Kendall went into the dressing room. Moments later she just stared. The beadwork and pearls were magnificent. She indeed felt like Cinderella. And she could imagine herself walking down an aisle toward Decker. The image was vivid, with Decker so handsome in a tuxedo and her own heart beating with sexual attraction. Not love.

Her excitement waned just then.

She should just take this off and give it back to the clerk and leave the shop. Tell her mother to back off too.

But instead, she left the little room with nerves churning her stomach.

As soon as Marion saw her, her mouth dropped open and her blue eyes seemed to gobble up the sight of Kendall. The dress was that magical.

"Oh, sweetie," her mother said. "You look absolutely stunning."

"You do look beautiful," the clerk concurred. "I've never helped anyone who found the perfect dress for them in such a short amount of time."

Despite her inner turmoil, Kendall did feel like a princess in this dress. It was okay to enjoy this. She did not have to think about the end of the month and what it would bring, not yet. "Maybe I'll spend more time on the veil," she said.

"We'll take the dress," her mother said.

Kendall felt tugged along by an invisible force, pushed ever closer to some unknown precipice. Would she be carried on clouds when she reached it or would she fall to a rocky bottom?

She changed and gave the gown to the clerk. Her mother paid, even though she really didn't need to. The dress was very expensive but Kendall could afford it with her trust fund. Her mother was traditional that way.

She left the shop with her mother smiling all the way.

As she walked toward their sedan, where the driver waited at the rear door, Kendall noticed a man sitting in a parked car across the street, watching them. She didn't recognize him. Wearing dark sunglasses and a black beanie, he looked like a big man, with his shoulders above the back of the seat and his head topping the headrest. His arms were large, as well.

Although she couldn't see his eyes, she could tell he looked right at them, or maybe only her. His mouth remained in a flat line.

"Who is that?" she asked.

Her mother looked across the street, stopping at the sedan. "I don't know."

"He's staring at us."

Her mother climbed into the back of the sedan and Kendall followed.

"He's staring at you, not me," her mother said, adjusting herself on the other side of the car.

"In a creepy way."

"He was probably just noticing a pretty woman."

Kendall wasn't so sure. She had a feeling he wasn't looking at her for her looks. Maybe he'd watched a strange woman come out of a bridal shop and had his own thoughts on that. Maybe he'd been dumped by a woman or his bride-to-be changed her mind. Who knew?

What other reason would a man have to park along the street and watch her? Kendall had no enemies.

Then why did she have this bad feeling?

She glanced back as their driver pulled out into traffic. The other car turned out onto the street and made a U-turn.

"What's the matter, sweetheart?" her mother asked, looking back like Kendall was.

"That car."

"It's that same man," Marion said. "Is he following you?"

The driver glanced in his rearview mirror. Kendall was glad he'd listened and was now alert to the potential danger. She glanced back again. The other car stayed three cars back but followed them down Main Street. As the town faded away and they headed back up the mountain toward home, the car remained behind them.

The driver didn't try to lose the other vehicle. Kendall wondered if that was a mistake. Would they lead the man to their home?

As they approached the turn to the road that would lead to their property, Kendall and her mother watched through the rear window. Their driver made the turn.

Kendall's heart pounded as the other car neared the turn. He didn't appear to slow and she breathed a sigh of relief when the driver passed on by without so much as a glance their way.

Kendall faced forward and leaned back against the seat.

"You sure are jumpy," her mother said.

"Maybe it's just the day. Buying a wedding dress is kind of a monumental event." Or maybe she hadn't imagined the man watching her and maybe he had deliberately followed them. Was it a message? But why on earth would a stranger be after her?

After hugging her mother goodbye, she got out of the car when it stopped by her house.

She locked the door and set the alarm, not understanding why she still felt so unsettled. She removed her jacket and other winter clothes and started farther into her house when the doorbell rang.

She stopped and stiffened. Could that driver have turned around and driven up the road and found her? She didn't see how. There were other driveways along the road they'd turned onto. Turning to the door, she went there and cautiously peeked out the side window. A florist stood there, holding a beautiful bouquet of wildflowers and a stuffed wolf. Instantly lighter of heart, she disarmed the alarm and opened the door.

"For you, ma'am," the middle-aged man in a baseball cap and a maroon puff jacket said.

She took the flowers and then the wolf. "Thank you."

The wolf felt soft and furry and the flowers wafted a sweet summery scent, a refreshing difference from the chill in the air today.

Closing and locking the door and rearming the security system, she took the stuffed animal and the flowers and left the entry, passing white-and-dark-wood-trimmed stairs and a console table. In the spacious, high-ceilinged living room, she went to the seating area, which was furnished with off-white chairs and a sectional sofa around a rectangular wooden coffee table.

Smiling to herself, she put the flowers on the coffee table and inspected the wolf, thinking this quite a creative gift. Looking for a card, she found it in the flowers.

Dinner was nice, but just a taste. I'll have a car pick you up at seven for another. Just you and me this time. Formal attire. D.

He'd gotten her wildflowers because she'd told him she loved the outdoors and he'd gotten her the wolf because she'd told him about the pack she'd spotted. How very thoughtful of him. She hadn't expected that.

Nevertheless, she wasn't sure if she liked his boldness. What if she had plans tonight? Did he expect her to drop everything just to go out with him? She'd have to ask. One thing she'd establish right from the start— she would not change her life to suit his schedule or his business aspirations. She had her standards and she would not compromise herself for him. He had to respect her.

Would he?

Chapter 4

Decker hadn't heard from Kendall, so he assumed she'd be ready when he had his car pick her up. He waited for her in the Columbine off the main lobby of The Lodge, where he'd reserved a section just for them. He had warned the staff to be at their top performance. Tonight he wore a suit and tie. He couldn't wait to see what Kendall had decided to wear, although she would look great in anything, even if she showed up in jeans just to spite him.

He received a text indicating Kendall had arrived. He stood with his hands clasped behind his back; soft jazz music played. No center candle tonight, instead, a brass table lamp. The small bar had a bartender who waited in his suit and tie. Decker had put them in a room often reserved for moderately large dinner parties. The two double-door-sized archway entries had glass French doors with draperies for privacy that he'd ordered closed, but the lights from the start of the gondola could still be seen from here.

He spotted Kendall walking toward him and froze for a second as her beauty dazzled him. Adorned, in a simple long black dress that V'd modestly at the bodice, it complimented her tall, graceful physique beautifully. She wore a sapphire necklace and matching earrings and had put her long blond hair up.

"You look radiant," he said, lifting her hand to his lips to plant a soft kiss along it as he had the other time.

Behind her, one of the waitstaff closed the French doors.

"You did say formal," Kendall said.

Straightening, he thought he detected a slight edge to her tone. "You could have come in jeans and I wouldn't have minded."

"You could have *asked* me to dinner instead of summoning me."

Oh, yes, definitely an edge. "I wouldn't call it summoning. Charming you into joining me, perhaps." She'd taken offense.

"It was presumptuous of you to assume I wouldn't have any other plans and if I did, that I'd change them."

He grunted, trying to smother a laugh. He would never presume anything of her. "Actually, I was sure you'd turn me down. When I didn't get a call, I got excited."

He saw her immediately soften. "Okay, you've redeemed yourself." She smiled. "Thank you for the flowers and the wolf. They were very considerate gifts."

"As was my intention." He indicated for her to join him at the bar.

She preceded him there, giving him a view of the scooping back of her dress and the curves it accentuated.

Champagne in hand, she faced him as he took a glass from the bartender.

"Do you have another elegant dinner planned?" she asked, taking a sip.

"Of course."

She moved away from the bar and went to the windows. He followed.

"Do you do this for all your girlfriends?"

He quirked a brow. "Are you my girlfriend or my fiancée?"

She glanced at him without replying.

"No," he said.

"Why are you trying so hard?" she asked.

"Because I want you to marry me."

With another glance, this one quicker and more uncertain, she turned and wandered into the space between the table and the bar.

"You fit me." He went to stand behind her, giving her plenty of distance to adjust to his blunt announcement. "You have a career you love. You come from a family that's similar to mine. And I get the feeling you want a no-fuss relationship as much as I do. I already know you're a great kisser. The only thing I don't know is if you want children."

Slowly she faced him, not as rattled. "No fuss?"

"We both want to continue to pursue our careers without worry that the other will walk away due to lack of understanding."

"Okay, but I'm not sure I want a relationship where I never spend any time with the person I'm with."

Had he gotten that wrong about her? She hadn't struck him as a woman who'd complain when her man didn't pay enough attention to her.

"We'd spend plenty of time together. We'd just have to work around our schedules, that's all."

That seemed to placate her. She continued to look at him and he fell into the spectacular blue of her eyes.

"Aside from the suddenness, what's holding you back from committing to marriage?" he asked. She was far too cautious to take marriage to him seriously. Yet.

"Remember that man I told you about?"

The jerk she'd caught with another woman? "Yes."

"That's why."

"You want my assurance that I'll never cheat? You have it. That's not my style. I'd divorce you before it came to that."

"Gee, that's comforting."

He chuckled. "I doubt I'd ever have a reason to divorce a woman like you. I'd have to be an idiot to do that."

"How can you be so sure when you barely know me?"

"I have a pretty strong feeling on the matter."

She met his eyes a moment and then went to the dining table to set down her glass. He waited for her to turn.

"It's more than that," she confided, bracing her hands on the back of a chair. "I loved him. His betrayal and the rude awakening that I never saw it coming made me withdraw from men. I like relationships that don't threaten to make me feel too much."

He failed to follow her meaning. Did she think she would feel too much with him…or did she worry she'd marry him because she knew she *wouldn't* feel too much?

He suspected it was both, but more of the latter. "Then it's good you won't feel threatened by marrying me. Whatever comes after that will happen on its own and in time." Whether they truly fell in love would remain an unknown until after they married. He saw that as a bonus. If they fell in love, great, but if not, they'd still have a solid companionship.

A slow smile emerged on her pretty face. "I like that. A lot."

"Good." He stepped closer and took her hands. "Let's dance." The jazz song had a perfect rhythm for romance.

She followed him into a dance and asked, "Aside from your excuse of being too busy to find love, does this arrangement appeal to you because of that woman who left you for another?"

"Women. Plural. I haven't been able to find any woman who could tolerate my schedule."

"How do you know I will?" she murmured.

He couldn't read her very well, but he thought she had concerns over whether she'd need more from him than he could give. "I suppose I don't. It's that feeling I have. I think we can make it work."

She gazed up at him, seeming satisfied with this heart-to-heart they'd just had. Good. She'd be all in then and he could focus on work. He still wasn't finished wooing her, though. He had to be sure he could secure this marriage.

"I do want children," she said out of the blue, as though capping off the discussion.

"That's good. I do too."

"You want a family but you work sixty hours a week? How is that going to work?"

"Work from home more."

She laughed. "You might as well hire a nanny."

"If we need to we will. But if you're worried we won't spend time as a family, I promise you we will." It might not be every night, but they'd have quality time together, especially after he was promoted to CEO and didn't have to constantly stroke his father's ego. Certainly after he inherited the entire business.

Kendall moved within his arms, relaxed and content, and Decker looked forward to another fantastic evening with her—one step closer to sealing the deal.

Kendall appreciated Decker's candor, but she still wasn't ready to commit to a hasty wedding. Not with her and Decker's fathers both overzealous to merge families and money. All business to them, but this involved her personal future. She didn't care about any business deal. Decker definitely intrigued her and she did feel sparks with him, but she wouldn't sacrifice herself for anyone, not even her father.

For dinner tonight, Decker had presented her with

a delicious mushroom soup followed by oysters with more champagne and also some caviar. The third course was ahi tuna tartare with avocado, crispy shallots and a soy-sesame dressing. The fourth was sea bass with a white wine cream sauce, and asparagus with sliced black truffles. The main and last course before dessert was filet mignon with crab and spinach in a béarnaise sauce. Decker was going to turn her into a real food connoisseur.

After another culinary work of art and flavors, she joined him for coffee in a small, historically decorated room, a lounge on an upper level of the lodge and, according to Decker, near his bedroom suite. She wasn't sure why he'd told her that. Did he hope to get her in bed tonight?

"What would you like to do for our next date?" he asked as he sat beside her on the sofa. He'd removed is jacket and draped it over a chair in the room.

Hm…she had to think of something good, something that would put him to the test to see if they'd be compatible. Kendall thought of her beloved wolves. Maybe she'd take him with her to watch them—if they'd still be there. Wolves traveled long distances and over a wide range. They could be where they were this summer and gone by fall, never to be seen again by human eyes.

"Why don't we start with a hike?" she suggested.

"Start?"

"Yes."

"Do I need to prove myself to you?"

She smiled, enjoying the flirtation. "Maybe."

When he put his arm along the back of the sofa, she

felt the chemistry change between them. He put his finger beneath her chin and guided her to tip her head up. She complied, too curious and warm to resist.

"You're so beautiful. Your smile captivates me," he murmured.

"Your eyes captivate me." A lot more about him captivated her. His thick dark hair, his tall muscular physique.

He leaned forward and kissed her, a feathery-light touch that mingled with warm breath and made her feel all shivery like that first time, only stronger. When he withdrew a fraction and she opened her eyes to see his burning back at her, she slipped further into passion. He might succeed in getting her into bed tonight. As soon as that thought came, reason returned and she pulled back awkwardly.

"I'm sorry, was that...? I figured, after that first kiss, we should try it again."

She smiled. "It was pretty good. I'm just not so sure about what follows."

He grinned back at her. "How about a movie?" He stood and seemed just as awkward as her. Retrieving a remote, he turned on a big screen TV hanging on the wall above a gas fireplace. No one else was in the lounge. He must have reserved it just for them.

He chose a clever animated movie, something Kendall didn't think either of them would actually watch but would help lighten the mood. Not that it would tame the sensation of that breathtaking kiss.

Kendall was aware of every move Decker made, the way he walked back to her and bent to put the remote on the coffee table, the way he lowered himself down onto the sofa. He sat close, whether intentional or unintentional, Kendall didn't know.

The movie began but Kendall couldn't stop her hyperawareness of Decker. She let herself take in his knee, sloping up to a hard, muscular thigh that touched her leg. Her heart rate kicked up as her eyes drifted upward, to where his pants seamed at his crotch, subtle hints to what lay beneath teasing her feminine senses. She wanted to reach out and run her hands over his flat abdomen to see if it was as ripped as it seemed. His dress shirt stretched over the panels of his chest muscles, drawing her desire in that direction. With his arm once again stretched out behind her, his shoulder bulged.

His square jaw had faint signs of dark stubble and his lips were together, soft and unsmiling. Black hair wisped around his ear and flirted with his collar. His cheekbones were slightly angular and his nose flaring just right. She followed the straight line up to his eyes and found the dark, smoldering orbs watching her.

Her breath quickened.

Decker reached up and sank his fingers into her updo, picking out the clasps until her hair fell down. He fingered the wavy blond strands, arranging them so they draped over her shoulder. Then he took his time looking at her, his gaze traveling hotly over her face and down for a top view of her cleavage.

The intense heat building between them told Kendall exactly where this was headed. Strangely, she had no desire to stop it. Rather, she wanted to experience this. The magic of this arousing feeling couldn't be denied.

She had taken care of birth control so she had nothing to worry about other than going on an intimate adventure with a man who had always fascinated her.

Decker leaned in, holding the back of her neck and kissing her with more force. She moved her mouth with his, felt his warm, impassioned breaths and splayed her palms against his chest as she had longed to do. His pecs were as hard as she imagined. Sliding her hands outward, she reveled in the feel of his shoulders and biceps, going back to his chest, staying there a while before roaming up again to his shoulders. She hung on for dear life as the kiss grew even more feverish.

Kendall realized she now lay on her back on the sofa, but she didn't care. This would do. She just had to have him.

She loosened his tie as he put his hands on her breasts, straddling her with one knee on the sofa and his other foot on the floor. Pulling the tie over his head, she tossed it aside. He reached for the hem of her dress and pulled it up. She lifted her hips to aid him and then rose up so he could pull it over her head, sending the soft, silky material pooling to the floor near his tie.

Kendall shivered with anticipation as Decker viewed her body hungrily. She wore lacy black underwear and a matching bra. When she'd put them on she hadn't planned on him seeing them tonight—she just felt sexy wearing them—and mischievous keeping it to herself. Her secret from him that was now out in the open.

He hastily unbuttoned his shirt.

Kendall rested her arms above her head and watched him. Words would ruin this. The silence worked like a charm, not allowing anything to stand in their way of satisfying a carnal curiosity.

When he revealed his chest and abs, she shivered with desire again. He had a sexy body. He must think the same of hers because his eyes all but devoured her whole.

He threw his shirt onto the floor and went to work on his pants and his shoes, never moving his gaze off her. In his boxer briefs, Kendall could see the hard ridge of him. Heat flared as he removed them and then came to her. Putting one knee on the sofa, he hooked two fingers beneath the edge of her black lace panties and slowly slid them off.

She opened her knees to make room for him to kneel on the sofa. Then he came down on her, kissing her hard. She moved her hands over him, down his back to his rear and up again. Unclasping her bra, he parted the material to reveal her breasts. He had to take several seconds just to stare.

"So beautiful."

His raspy voice and the hot, hungry look in his eyes gave her as much enjoyment as he obviously received seeing her bareness.

"So are you."

His eyes lifted to meet hers for a moment before he put his mouth on her, flicking her nipple.

Kendal lifted her hips to urge him on.

He pressed back but moved his attention to her other breast. She'd go out of her mind with lust if he didn't take care of her. She arched again, unable to stifle a moan.

"Decker. Now," she said, drowning in passion and needing him so much.

He answered with a gruff sound and probed for her. Finding her, he sank into her wetness. Kendall dug her head back against the sofa with another moan, this one louder.

Grunting his pleasure, Decker began moving, excruciatingly slow. He shook with his effort to maintain control. She felt her own trembling begin. She gripped his arms and became transfixed by his eyes looking into hers.

With each withdrawal and penetration, her breath came harder. On the next deep stroke, he ground hard against her, pausing.

"Don't stop," she whispered urgently.

"Kendall."

"Please."

He withdrew and thrust hard and repeated the movement a few more times, giving her what she needed.

Kendall cried out with her release, a dynamite explosion that blinded her for a moment. She was vaguely aware of his own sounds and then he collapsed onto her.

Both of them breathed heavily.

"Holy God," Kendall gasped. "What was that?"

"You have to marry me for sure now," he said.

Kendall dressed, the escape from reality no longer providing her solace. The magnitude of how good they were together haunted her now. So did his comment. He wanted to marry her more than ever, not for love, but for business and the added bonus of great sex.

"I should get going." She needed time alone to process all of this.

He'd put on his jeans and looked at her. "You want to leave?"

"I need to get home."

"Why? I think you should move in with me."

"No." She wasn't ready for that.

"At least stay the night, then." Closing the distance between them, he towered over her, crowding her space.

She stepped back. "I really need to go home."

He studied her a moment. "What's the matter?"

"Nothing."

Again, he studied her. "Did that scare you?"

Scare her? More like terrified her. What if she fell in love with him? She was a business deal to him.

"No," she lied.

"Yes." He stroked his thumb along her jaw. "Don't be."

She stepped back. "I'm not afraid."

He stared at her, his expression clearly saying he didn't believe her. "I'm not going anywhere. I won't hurt you, Kendall. You can trust me."

Words, just words. The thing about the future was nobody knew what lurked there.

"I'll call you in a few days." She turned and headed for the door.

"Wait." He caught up to her. "A few days?"

"I need time, Decker."

"No, you need more of what we just did tonight." He took hold of her arm and stopped her.

Reluctantly she looked up at his handsome face.

"You need to spend more time with me," he said.

"For how long, Decker? Until we're married and you

absorb yourself in work and I become nothing more than a bed partner?" She wished she had never said that.

"You are scared. I get that, really I do. But there's nothing to worry about." He gently clasped her shoulders and smiled down at her. "You'll be living with me and I'll see you every day. Every morning and every night, you'll be by my side."

She had a hard time imagining that when he'd be working so many hours. She'd be in bed asleep when he got home, or close to it. And why was she so worried about that? Did she really need him so close all the time? Why did she feel so insecure? Maybe it wasn't insecurity. Maybe it was this problem she had with marrying a man she didn't love and who didn't love her.

She reminded herself that she'd been burned in love before and this arrangement was safe. If he never loved her, he'd still be hers and she would never be hurt by him. He might claim now that he'd never hurt her, but it would be impossible to hurt her if she didn't love him.

But what if she did fall in love with him? That same question came back to slap her.

"Take tonight. Tomorrow let's talk. The following day, I want you to spend the night with me."

The command sent a flash of heated desire through her. But she didn't like his bossiness. "I'll think about it."

He hooked his arm around her and pulled her against him. "I really do want you to stay the night with me, Kendall." He kissed her, firm and warm and with a tickle of his tongue, reminding her how potent they were together.

Would she be able to say no to him? Would she be able to say no to more of what had transpired tonight?

"I don't think that's a good idea." She eased away from him and he didn't stop her.

After observing her a moment, he used his phone to call for a car.

He walked with her to the elevators and rode that down to the lobby and the front entrance. She saw the sedan pulling up to the front.

"Thank you for a lovely dinner and..." What could she say? For giving her hot, steamy sex and making her feel like a million bucks?

"I'll call you," he said softly.

She nodded and walked toward the waiting car.

On the short ride back to her house, Kendall could think of nothing but Decker. She couldn't get over how different he was from what she'd expected. Even after growing up amid great wealth and continuing on in his father's footsteps, he had more honor and integrity than any other man she'd ever met. She couldn't give any examples to support that assessment. It was more of a gut feeling than anything, and the way they'd connected over that first dinner and again tonight.

His boldness bothered her but she had to admit she preferred a straight-shooting man than one telling her what she wanted to hear.

As the driver turned onto the road leading to her driveway, she noticed lights shining behind them. Twisting, she saw a car about a hundred yards behind. There were not many houses off this road. She couldn't tell what kind of car it was or how many people were inside.

Should she tell the driver to stop? She didn't want to lead a stranger to her house. What if the driver of that car was the same man watching her earlier today?

If it was that man, and he was following her, he already knew which road to turn on. How much more would it take for him to find her house?

"Is that car following us?" she asked the driver.

He looked in the rearview mirror. "I don't think so, ma'am. I didn't notice anyone on the highway."

He resumed driving, unconcerned if not a little curious over her odd question.

She looked back as the driver turned onto her driveway. She watched the car pass. Through the darkness she couldn't tell if it was the same car. She thought it could be, though.

Chapter 5

A few days later, Kendall finished up at the office and left to go grab some lunch at her favorite restaurant in town that made the best salads. She and her father had finished a meeting on the latest numbers generated from beetle kill pine. Work had taken her mind off Decker, but now that she stepped out into the crisp air, he was back to taking up space in her mind.

Vaguely seeing a man leaning against a car with his arms folded, Kendall stopped short when recognition hit her.

Decker grinned, eyes hidden by sunglasses. She had avoided his phone calls and now he'd intercepted her at the office.

Slowly she went to him. "What are you doing here?"

"Picking you up for lunch." He opened the back door

of the tinted-windowed sedan. "Your dad told me you had a meeting right before lunch and you had plans to go to The Toss."

"He did, did he?" She climbed into the sedan, scooting over to make room for him.

She couldn't help feeling tickled that he'd surprised her.

"How's your day at work going?" Decker asked.

"Good. Beetle kill inventory is improving profits. I'm going to go check on my wolf pack tomorrow." She angled toward him so she'd get a good look at his face when she asked a question. "What about you? How is it that you can take time out of your busy day for me?"

"I'll always make time for you, darling."

Hm. Already calling her *darling*. And she debated whether he'd always make time for her. He made extra effort now to get her to the altar but once they were married would he devote most of his time and energy at The Lodge? Instinct said a resounding yes. She couldn't help feeling like a business deal.

"Do you want company when you go check on your wolf pack? I've never done anything like that."

Kendall coveted her time in the wilderness and was protective of the wolves. "They'll be a sight to see for sure. They're in a good part of the forest, with plenty of prey."

"How big is the pack?"

"There are six of them. The mating pair probably dispersed from their birth pack and had two or three litters so they're probably about four or five years old."

"I'd love to see them. Not many people have an opportunity to see something like that."

"Well, if you behave and do what I say, I suppose I can trust you to come with me."

He chuckled. "I'll behave."

The driver parked the sedan in front of The Toss in a parallel parking space.

She climbed out and Decker waited with an offered hand on the sidewalk. As she rounded the rear of the sedan, she noticed the same car she'd seen with her mother outside of the bridal shop. It was parked a few spaces behind the sedan. The man inside watched her, wearing sunglasses again. She stopped to get a closer look. He had dark hair, shoulder length, and she'd guess he was around six feet tall and appeared to be fairly well built.

The driver pulled out into the street and passed without looking at her again. Kendall turned in a half circle as she watched the car disappear down the street.

"Someone you know?" Decker asked.

She faced him. "No."

He took her hand and studied her as they walked toward the restaurant doors. "Is something wrong?"

She tried to shake it off. "No." Should she tell him about the stranger? She wasn't even sure if she had anything to worry about.

"Is that man bothering you?" Decker asked with a frown.

"Kendall Hadley, is that you?" a woman murmured, interrupting Decker's question and sparing Kendall from having to answer.

Looking up, she saw Karen Evanston coming out of the restaurant. She hadn't seen her since high school. Around five-seven with long dark hair and blue eyes that were darker than Kendall's, she hadn't changed much.

"Hi!" Kendall hugged her old friend.

"I heard you were back." Karen reclined and looked away from her to glance at Decker. "Why haven't you called?"

"I'm sorry. I've just been busy. I planned to see if we could get together for lunch sometime."

"Let's do plan something. I've missed you. You're working for your dad now?"

"Yes."

"I always envied how close you were to your parents."

"Must be an only child thing," Kendall said.

Her friend glanced once again at Decker.

"This is Decker Colton," Kendall said.

"So, all the rumors are true?" Karen's eyes brightened with excitement. "You're getting married?"

"Well—"

"Yes, we are," Decker said.

"An...*arranged* marriage?" Karen hesitantly said. "That doesn't sound like you."

"It's not really an arranged marriage. Nobody is forcing me. And we haven't officially decided."

"We've set a date," Decker interjected with a grin.

Karen looked on in amusement. "Yikes. That's pretty quick. How did this all come about?"

"Our parents thought we would be a good match," Kendall answered.

"That sounds so…medieval." Karen laughed lightly, clearly thrilled with this juicy bit of news. "And maybe romantic. I remember you two from high school. I always wondered why you never got together back then, even though Kendall wasn't popular. None of us were."

Apparently a lot of people thought that, those who knew them that long.

"I married Ted Nelson," she added.

Ted Nelson had been one of the biggest nerds in school. Karen hadn't been into academics. She was more of a social creature.

"Wow," Kendall said.

"Yeah. He's a spacecraft engineer. I stay home with the kids. We have two." She dug into her purse and produced her phone and navigated to a photo of two adorable kids. "Four and two."

Kendall took another look at her old friend. In a beige dress and holding a designer purse, she was apparently living well. Her husband must make a good living. Kendall had never doubted Ted would be successful.

"They're cute," Kendall said, smiling warmly.

"Funny, I always thought you would end up with someone like Ted. I suppose you feel more comfortable with your own kind."

Her smile faded. Kendall had always suspected Karen had been jealous of her wealthy upbringing.

"Decker isn't like his father," she said, glancing over at Decker's entertained observation.

"No, I meant money."

"You don't seem to be struggling much."

Karen smiled wide. "No, but we aren't millionaires."

Kendall didn't respond. What could she say?

With somewhat of a haughty look, Karen said, "Well, it was good to see you again, Kendall. I should get going. The kids are with their nanny."

Kendall said goodbye and watched her friend walk down the sidewalk with a high head.

"If the rumors haven't spread like wildfire yet, they will now," Kendall said.

"I'm not worried about that. What does concern me is that man in the car. You seemed to recognize him."

Kendall sighed. Apparently he wasn't going to let her get away with not telling him something. The thing was, she didn't know if there was anything to tell.

"I thought he was parked outside the bridal shop my mother and I went to the other day," she said. "Maybe I imagined it."

"Maybe you didn't."

That disturbed her. "Why would someone be watching me?"

"Perhaps to track your movements. Get to know your patterns. Discover where you live."

"But *why*?" She could think of no one who would do that. She had no enemies. Any man she broke up with hadn't been hurt. It had to be random. Some creep who'd seen her and now had a fixation on her.

"One more reason you should move in with me."

"He hasn't done anything. He's just a stalker."

"*Just* a stalker?" he bit out. "We should report him to the police."

"And tell them what, Decker? I don't even know who the man is."

"You can describe him. What kind of car is he in?"

She furrowed her brow in concentration. "It was older, like a faded tan four-door Taurus or something."

"That's distinctive. How old? Eighties? Nineties?"

"Probably nineties," she answered.

"All right. We'll tell the police after lunch and then tomorrow after you take me hiking to see your wolves, then you're coming to stay with me."

"I am not."

"One night."

She hesitated. They'd already had sex. What harm would it do to stay one more night with him? While she still didn't like his forcefulness, the temptation won her over.

"I'll think about it," she said.

"That's what I like to hear." He pulled her into his arms and dropped a tender kiss on her forehead. "I just want to keep you safe, that's all."

"I know," she murmured, warmth flooding through her at the genuine concern in his voice.

"And I'm also not opposed to testing out this arrangement, either. I think we need more practice."

At his teasing tone and look in his eyes, Kendall gave him a soft slap on his chest. "Whoa there, big fella."

"Don't you want to do some more testing?" he asked. She almost blurted that she did. "Maybe."

"I'll take a maybe."

The next morning, Decker picked Kendall up in a Jeep Grand Cherokee. And not just *any* Cherokee. This was the seven-hundred-horsepower SUV, worth the vicinity of ninety-nine thousand dollars. He liked his automobiles and liked even more how Kendall appreciated its beauty, a sleek medium-dark blue machine with the tires that looked like paws for the road. She walked all the way around it while he waited at the passenger door.

At the passenger door, she stopped. "Very impressive."

"Who says four-wheeling can't be done in luxury."

She sank down onto the plush gray leather seat and he shut her door and went around to the driver's side.

Inside, he started driving. "Any sign of your secret admirer?"

The lightness in her expression faded some. "No. I didn't get much sleep last night."

He would like to remedy that.

Decker drove on a narrow, somewhat rugged dirt road to a small parking area at the head of a hiking trial, relatively near where Kendall had seen the wolves. As they emerged from the vehicle, she told him they'd hike for about a mile and then get off the trail. From there she'd estimated it was another three or four miles.

"They roam a lot," she explained, "but their den must be close to this location because I've seen them in the area more than once."

She went on to say that wolves roamed great distances while hunting for food.

"Even near people?" Decker asked. "How busy is this trail?"

"I doubt they ever get near this trail," she answered. "They must know humans are present."

He followed behind, enjoying the view of her rear in her breathable taupe pants. She carried a backpack and so did he, filled with all the necessities of a day hike. The weather had cooperated. They had a clear blue sky beyond the canopy of pine trees and a forecasted upper-fifty-degree high for the day. He'd be removing his jacket before long.

They had the trail to themselves, as well. No other cars had been in the parking area. This trail was pretty remote and steep in some places.

In a clearing, Kendall stopped and looked around. "Wind is gentle and coming from the southwest. We need to stay downwind from them."

"They've never seen you?"

"No. I don't want them to." That made sense. Wolves were solitary creatures aside from their close-knit pack.

The next time she stopped, she inspected a patch of aspen trees and then veered off the trail. She kept studying the landscape, changing course every so often.

"Can I ask you something?" He had to know why she'd agreed to set a wedding day but was so reluctant to stay the night with him. Granted, he'd been the one to set the date, but she hadn't disagreed that night at his parents' mansion. She'd looked a bit startled but hadn't said a thing. And when she had left, he'd never forget the way she'd looked back at him as she went through the front doors, as though tantalized.

"Sure." She didn't turn back to look at him as she continued to hike.

"What was that man like who you lived with after college?"

"Gabe? He was smart and quiet."

"Quiet?"

"Yeah. We didn't talk much. I mean, we did, but he wasn't the kind to carry on long conversations, a 'just the facts' kind of person."

"What did you have in common?"

"We had similar degrees in college. We both loved wildlife and preserving the environment. He cared about things like that just the way I did." She hiked without talking a few steps. "I still don't know what went wrong."

"Did he tell you he loved you?" he asked.

"Yes."

"Did you believe him?"

"Yes."

"He must have loved you then." Decker thought a moment. "What did the two of you do together? For fun."

"We did things like this and we went to museums and festivals. We did a lot together. He seemed to really understand me."

He could tell it bothered her not to know what had caused Gabe to stray. "Did he give you a reason?"

She shook her head. "Not really. He said he made a mistake sleeping with the other woman, that it didn't mean anything." She hiked a few more steps. "But I knew I could never forgive him, and even if I could, it would never be the same again."

Decker could relate to that.

"Was he intimidated by your family's wealth?" he asked.

With that she stopped and turned to face him. "He said he wasn't."

"Saying and believing are two different things." Decker wouldn't be surprised if that had been a key factor in their demise. "Be grateful it ended when it did. Gabe may have loved you but he might not have never adjusted to you having more money than he'd ever make in a lifetime."

"But he wasn't…" She averted her face.

"What was his upbringing like?" Decker asked.

Now Kendall lowered her head. "He grew up poor." She lifted her head and met his eyes. "Single mom. Never knew his father. That's why he worked so hard to put himself through college, so he could line himself up with a good-paying job and never be poor again. I admired him for that."

"And you still should. Unless he was only using you for money. I've run into that a few times. Eventually I learned how to recognize the signs."

Kendall didn't respond right away, as though mulling that over. Then she said, "No." She shook her head. "I don't believe he was that kind of man."

"Then you're lucky. Hang on to the good memories of him and forget the bad."

She looked into his eyes some more, her demeanor softening with appreciation. "You're pretty insightful, Decker Colton."

"Naw, just experienced with human nature."

With a slight smile she glanced back at him as she continued to hike.

About a mile and a half later, Kendall halted and

stooped. When Decker came to her side, he saw wolf tracks in the snow.

"We need to proceed slowly," she said.

He followed her lead, excited to see live gray wolves. He'd be as quiet as a field mouse to have that privilege.

Kendall came to the top of a hill and stayed behind a group of trees and a boulder. She stopped and lifted her hand. Decker waited for her go ahead. Had she spotted the wolves? He looked through the trees and didn't see anything. He stopped behind her and looked over her shoulder. In the distance, a group of gray wolves had gathered on a patch slope exposed to the sun where the snow had melted. The largest of the six were higher up the slope, one lying on dead grass and the other standing above, as though keeping watch.

Two of the smaller wolves growled and nipped and bounded into each other for some rough play. The other two finished eating a carcass the pack must have killed.

"The biggest ones are the mated pair," Kendall whispered. "The female is lying down. The others are their offspring."

The wolves were a family unit. Decker watched the two youngest, the smallest of the pack, stop playing to go over to the carcass. The other two let them take bites. He imagined his and Kendall's kids playing and was surprised by the strength of his desire to one day witness that.

The male sniffed the air, his head in Kendall and Decker's direction.

Decker watched the magnificent creature walk toward them, smelling the air. Then his head lowered and he growled, baring teeth. The female sprang to her feet and looked in their direction.

"Don't move," she cautioned.

Kendall didn't have to worry. He'd rather not be attacked by a hundred-and-eighty-pound wolf. This male looked about five feet long and thirty-two inches tall at the shoulder. He was huge. And healthy.

The female was smaller at about a hundred fifty, but she was just as impressive.

"They look like their thriving here," he whispered.

She nodded with a smile, not taking her eyes off the wolves.

The male trotted toward the carcass and the four offspring.

"We better go," Kendall said.

Reluctantly, Decker left the scene and noticed Kendall hiked farther away from the trail and not toward it.

"Where are we going?" He hoped they'd try for another view of the wolves.

"I just want to look around a little. I've suspected for some time that their den is somewhere near here." She scanned the landscape. "I'm pretty sure the female is pregnant."

He'd like to see her pregnant.

She stopped and pointed. "Look."

He stopped close to her and saw a large boulder in a stand of pine trees and aspen. But he was more aware of her. He turned his head and smelled her hair, wanting to run his hands through it and then turn her head and kiss her.

"It's their den," Kendall said, turning and seeing him looking at her.

A moment passed where he thought he would kiss her, but then she pointed.

"Look."

He did and saw a small opening at the base of the boulder. On a south-facing slope, the den would be drier and warmer.

"I wish we could get closer," she murmured.

She must not want to put the scent of humans anywhere near their den, especially since the female would be delivering a litter soon.

"This mating pair is young." She faced him. "Gray wolves live up to about thirteen years in the wild. This pair likely dispersed from their natal pack. Typically they disperse from fifty to a hundred miles from their natal pack."

"Why do they disperse?" he asked, admiring her passion for what she did.

"They're strong alphas. These two probably dispersed to find a mate and their own territory to start a new pack."

"How soon after we get married do you want to start having kids?" He knew it was an abrupt question, but he couldn't seem to stop himself.

Her mouth dropped open.

"All this talk about mating pairs is making my mind wander," he added.

That spread a smile over her face. "We can decide after we're married."

She started back down the mountain and he walked beside her.

"Why do wolves howl?" he asked to divert talk about kids.

"I'm not sure. I'm not sure if anyone could answer that with any certainty. It might be to signal territories. It might just be a check-in with other packs. I do know it's a myth that they howl at the moon."

He chuckled. "Only in fiction, huh."

"Only in fiction."

"We should take a break for lunch," he said.

He hadn't told her he had something special planned.

"Okay." She looked around.

"Let's hike back down a little ways and then stop."

"Okay. That'd be good. Farther from the pack."

"Yes."

Almost thirty minutes later, he spotted the portable gazebo and staff. He'd arranged for them to set up in an open area, far enough up the mountain so they'd get there by one or two in the afternoon, yet close enough to the parking area to make it easier to set up. They had SUVs and small trailers and it looked like they'd pulled it off just as he'd imagined.

"What is that?" Kendall asked. "Is someone having a party up here? That's odd. I've never seen that before."

"That's lunch," he said.

She stopped and gaped at him. "What?"

"It's our lunch. I hope you like lobster rolls with tarragon mayonnaise. We'll start with shrimp cocktail and a Caesar salad. I figured we'd be hungry."

She gaped at him some more. "You can stop pulling

out all the stops now, you know. I like you enough to keep seeing you."

"Yes, but do you like me enough to marry me at the end of the month?"

Without responding, she walked toward the gazebo.

He took that as a no, and he would not stop working hard to impress her.

Chapter 6

The following weekend, Kendall rose from Decker's McLaren sports car with her hand on his. Her flowing white cocktail gown slipped back from her knee where it parted high up on her left thigh and fell closed once she stood straight. Decker's eyes went to the deep V in the front of the sleeveless bodice. Soft pleats flared gently from the banded waist. He looked just as elegant in his dark suit and white tie.

"I still think you did this on purpose," she said with a coy smile.

"Plan a charity ball?" He chuckled. "Even I would need more time to plan that. No, this was my parents."

"Then Russ did this on purpose."

"Maybe. In any event, it will be a glamorous evening."

She could do without glamour, but it would be a great night, especially since the charity was for The Nature Conservancy. At ten thousand a plate, this fund-raiser would produce a significant amount. And she had been excited all day to show up on Decker's arm. Kind of a girlhood fantasy come to life, close to what she had imagined in high school. Only better.

As the valet took Decker's car, she took in the splendor of The Chateau, from the expansive garden, impeccably manicured but dormant now, to the large fountain with a tall statue of a woman with her arm arched above her head. Kendall's high heels clicked on the stone driveway that passed along the front of the massive architectural work of art of The Chateau. Towering columns flanked each side and several archways led to an elaborate front entrance.

A doorman opened one of the doors for them and Kendall stepped into the foyer. High overhead, arching beams reached from front to back and double circular staircases met at the second level. Plants in built-in boxes flourished in the lobby and another fountain gently splashed between the staircases.

She put her arm in Decker's as they walked to the conference center. The elite charity cocktail party would be held in The Chateau's grand ballroom.

The room sported glittering crystal chandeliers and white-linen-covered tables with a sizable crowd of formally clad men and women. Kendall could smell the giant pots of fresh flowers placed throughout the expansive room. An orchestra played at the far end and a few couples danced.

She recognized a few famous actors and actresses, laughing and having a good time. The press wasn't allowed inside these hallowed grounds. She also spotted a senator and his wife. Her parents couldn't make it tonight but she saw Russ and Mara heading their way.

"Brace yourself," Decker joked.

Petite and thin, Mara had to take twice as many strides as Russ with his tall frame. Her short blond hair had been styled into well-placed curls with pins that flattered her face and she wore diamond earrings. Her dark blue eyes sparkled with professionally applied makeup. Straying from her usual classic business attire, she wore a glittery silver gown.

Broad-shouldered and in a silky tuxedo Russ neared them beside Mara, his dark brown, graying hair combed smooth and his brown eyes shrewd as usual.

"Ah, Kendall." Russ took her in for a brief, impersonal hug. "You look radiant."

"That's a lovely gown," Mara said, sparkling in her silver sequins.

"Yours is too," Kendall said to be polite.

"Have you two been spending a lot of time together?" Russ asked.

"As much as possible," Decker replied. "Kendall showed me her pack of wild gray wolves the other day."

The way he looked at her warmed her and convinced her the pride she saw was genuine.

"Oh my, that sounds dangerous. Was it safe?" Mara looked Kendall over as though she'd lost her mind.

"We stayed a good distance away and were careful

not to disturb them. The last thing I want is to frighten them away from a healthy habitat," Kendall said.

"I would have been the frightened one." Mara turned to her son. "You aren't the outdoors type, are you, Decker? Your taste is more accustomed to what surrounds us now."

"I run a ski resort, mother."

"It's not just *any* ski resort."

No, it catered to the rich and famous. Mara clearly had trouble picturing her son in the wild.

"You would have been impressed," Kendall added. "I was."

Russ chuckled. "It's good to see the two of you getting along so well." He leaned in toward Decker. "Don't let anyone steal her from you, son."

"Kendall will stay where she wants." He turned warm eyes to her. "And that's right next to me."

Kendall wondered if he said that to make his father happy or if he was really that cocky. Was she a business deal to him as much as she was to his father? She didn't like being treated like that. Even if she went through with the wedding out of convenience, she refused to be a hot commodity.

"Decker!"

Kendall turned to see Skye Colton headed their way with a big, radiant smile. Younger sister of Decker's, the five-fourish, redheaded marketing manager had an energy about her. She rushed over and flew into her brother's arms. Decker had twin sisters: Skye and Phoebe. Kendall searched around for his adopted sister Sloane and didn't see her. Sloane and her brother, Fox, had been adopted by their Aunt Mara Colton and Russ.

"Hey, kiddo. It's been a while."

Skye leaned back. "Only because you work too much."

"I'm not working now."

"I see that." She stepped away and glanced at Kendall. "Sloane told me she talked to you about Dad wanting you to get married. And you agreed. I had to see to believe."

"When are the invitations going out?" Skye asked.

Kendall didn't say anything. She hadn't thought of invitations. They had no time. Then it occurred to her she hadn't thought to deny there'd be a wedding. Which meant what—that she wasn't as unsure as she'd originally thought? Yet how *could* she be sure in such a short period of time?

Before she started going crazy again with all the what-ifs, Kendall reminded herself why arranged marriage appealed to her. It was because she wouldn't get hurt if it didn't work out. She could minimize the sanctity of marriage and opt for the ease of divorce if things went south. And if things ended up working out—even if she and Decker didn't fall in love and just remained good companions—isn't that what she desired most?

Yes.

She realized Decker was waiting for her to say something. He was leaving it up to her. What a gentleman. Once again he surprised her with how considerate he was.

"I suppose we better get on it," she said.

Decker's reaction heated her in places best kept private. His eyes smoldered as he looked at her, a completely satisfied man—or a triumphant one.

"If you need help, Phoebe and I can handle that," Skye said. "All you have to do is give us a list of who you want to attend, Kendall. I pretty much know who to invite on Decker's side."

"Oh, that would be great if you did that," Kendall said, sincerely appreciating the offer. "With such a short amount of time, it's hard to stay on top of all that needs to be done."

"Dad already arranged the reception," Decker said. "It will be at the Colton Manor. Kendall and I haven't decided where the ceremony will take place." He looked at her again. "Actually, I don't know how you feel about a church wedding."

"Some churches are architecturally beautiful," she said. "I like the ones with the most interesting history. And style."

"There's a church in town that was built in the late eighteen hundreds," Skye said.

"I know the one you're talking about," Kendall said, loving the idea of a wedding there. "Let's do it!"

She felt genuinely excited. The church Skye mentioned was on the outskirts of town, small and preserved. The cemetery on the grounds was fenced in and full of flowering perennials. It had a small parklike front yard and a small gravel parking area. Very Kendall-like. She had no religious denomination but did believe in a higher power.

"Wait," she said to Decker. "How do you feel about a church wedding?"

"The same as you."

Was he lying? How did he really feel?

"I wouldn't get married in a church if I had an issue with it," he said as though answering her thoughts.

She could only stare at him, disbelieving they were having this conversation. He, obviously, enjoyed it immensely.

"What else do you need done?" Skye asked. "I can assign people to get everything handled."

"Um." Kendall decided to go with it. "Cake."

Skye drew back a bit. "Isn't that something you want to do?"

"I'm not big on sweets." She glanced at Decker. Was he? She saw no reaction from him. He didn't seem to react to much. He had a witty mind, but did not demonstrate much body language—other than when he reacted to her physically. Which she wouldn't complain about, least of all at this early stage.

"Pretty cakes aren't really my thing unless a guest at The Lodge wants one," he said wryly.

"Cake," Skye said. "Check. Next?" She began texting into her phone, no doubt assigning tasks to workers or associates.

"Guest book," Kendall said, "and flowers."

"Lots of flowers," Decker interjected.

"Of course."

"Will you have bridesmaids?" Skye asked.

"One." Kendall would have her closest friend from

high school and of course invite all her other friends. Again remembering Decker, she looked at him.

"Wyatt will be the best man," he told his sister.

"Okay." Skye stopped texting and smiled at Kendall then Decker. "That's enough for now." She grasped Kendall's hand. "Welcome to the family. I can't wait to get to know you."

Kendall smiled back. "Thanks. Me too."

Skye turned to her brother. "I'll call you. I'm going to go mingle."

"Okay, Skye. Thanks."

Skye rose up and planted a kiss to his cheek and said in a low tone that the music failed to drown out, "Don't let her get away."

The whole scene with Skye kept playing over in Decker's mind. Was Kendall really on board with the wedding now? The prospect kindled excitement.

He danced with her and fielded curious questions. Kendall had taken a big step tonight. He didn't want to scare her off with too much talk of their wedding.

"Come on," he finally said. "I want to show you something." Really he just wanted to be alone with her.

He took her hand and was glad when she didn't resist. Through the back of The Chateau, he led her past the oval garden and paved driveway to a path that in summer bloomed a profusion of color. He could have taken her to the indoor pool and accessed the springs from there, but he wanted to get her away from people.

He entered the gate leading to the outdoor portion of the pool.

"Natural spring water feeds this pool," he told her. The water is cooled before it flows into the hot tub and cooled more before it flows into the outdoor-indoor pool."

"Where does the water come from?"

"Scientists aren't exactly sure, but the water is believed to come from trapped groundwater heated by volcanic activity deep in the earth."

She looked at him in surprise. "The spring must be enormous."

He nodded. "Twenty-seven-hundred gallons of water flow to the surface every minute, some of it as hot as a hundred-twenty-five degrees. In the eighteen hundreds, the Ute Indians used this site as a healing and sacred place, calling it Yampah, meaning big medicine. Doc Holliday came here."

She nodded this time. "And died here."

He chuckled. She obviously had her doubts over the healing potential of the hot springs.

"The spring water dissolved limestone deposits in fault structures in the rock, leaving behind minerals that formed layers of travertine. It's the minerals that are believed to be therapeutic."

He reached the rock formation where the underground springs began. "I used to play here when I was a kid." He indicated the bathhouse. "Before that was renovated."

"Can you actually get down into the springs?"

"No, but you can explore three miles of vapor caves at three hundred vertical feet deep." Some of the passageways are not for the claustrophobic, but there are some very impressive stalactites and stalagmites."

"You've been there?"

He grinned. "Oh yeah, when I was about nineteen."

"Funny, I didn't peg you for an outdoorsman."

"Hello, ski resort."

She laughed lightly and sat on a bench that had a patchy view of city lights.

He sat beside her.

"I like to read, too. I read about an hour every night. Or morning if I get home too late. I like science or non-fiction overall."

"I read, too, but fiction. I get enough science at my day job."

He stood. "Come on. I want to show you something."

He took her hand and was glad she didn't pull away. He found another path, this one not traveled much, as his family had kept it a secret and didn't allow guests this far from the property.

He heard the water before they reached the small, natural spring. Solar lighting promised a lit late-night bath for those who wished one. He led Kendall through the trees and heard her intake of breath.

"Oh, it's beautiful." She left him to go to the edge of the steaming pool, crouching and sticking her finger into the water.

"It's naturally ninety-two degrees." Hot tub temperature. The water bubbled, minimally but it bubbled.

"I want to get in," she said.

He glanced back, not hearing the party, of course. Everyone was inside The Chateau. There were guests at the pool but that was a good distance from here. Unless someone from his family ventured this way, no one would be the wiser.

"Okay." He loosened his tie.

Kendall laughed and stood, kicking off her high heels and reaching up to undo the clasp holding the bodice of her dress around her neck. The weather had warmed today and wasn't too chilly now, although they would have to hurry to get into the spring water. This time of year in Colorado the weather could fluctuate quite a bit.

He removed his tie and jacket and draped them over a rectangular flat-topped rock his dad had installed. She stepped out of her dress, and stood before him in only her underwear. He had to stop moving, so arrested by her beauty, and then quickly undressed the rest of the way.

She removed her underwear and stepped down into the pool. His dad had hired someone to carve benches into the rock, and natural layers that had already been there served as steps. There had also been a metal grate installed where the crevasse opened below. He walked naked around to the other side, where a rock-enclosed storage space kept towels for this very purpose.

He removed two and placed them on a bench nearby, then stepped in across from her.

"I can see why you attract such an elite crowd," she said, sinking into the water just above her breasts and leaning back.

"Sometimes my parents do let famous people back here. But just occasionally. We all agreed early on that it's best kept a private thing."

"Yes." She closed her eyes. "I can smell the minerals."

It wasn't a sulfuric smell so much as it was like a salt bath.

When he came here, which wasn't often and usually by himself, he liked to imagine that somewhere deep, deep beneath was a plume of magma, churning and pressurized.

"When the groundwater comes into contact with the hot magma, it creates a phreatic explosion," he told Kendall. "I think that's what generates the circulation, bringing this slice of heaven to the surface."

"You seem to know a lot about how the springs formed," Kendall said.

"Maybe that's what I'd have done if I hadn't done what my dad wanted, gotten a geology degree along with a business degree and gone to work for some kind of environmental firm."

"It's not too late to go back to college. I know a lot of people our age who've done it."

"And leave all this?" He spread his hands out briefly.

She just smiled. "I think I'd have a hard time leaving this, as well."

He moved across the spring to sit beside her, stretching his arm out along the stone behind her. "I think I'd have a hard time leaving you."

Her eyes rolled toward him wryly. "You'd say anything to get me to marry you. Secure the deal?"

Was she testing him? He was trying very hard to secure this deal, but he wouldn't say just anything to win her for that reason. In fact, the more he analyzed what he'd said, the more he thought he meant exactly that. He truly believed they'd make a good pair. They didn't have to fall in love to be successful.

"Not *anything*," he said.

Her eyes warmed, her lids slowly closing and then opening as though in reaction to his sincerity.

He brushed a tendril of hair she'd left down from the artful updo she'd arranged and leaned closer to kiss her.

"You amaze me."

She angled her head as though wondering why he had said that.

"You come from such enormous wealth and yet you're so humble and caring," he murmured.

"My parents did something right," she joked.

"I'd say." He looked down her body and back up again, teasing.

"You always were a rake."

"I don't have time to be a rake anymore."

Maybe that was why he had agreed to his father arranging this marriage. He could tell she liked that he admitted to not womanizing anymore. Even though the reason was he worked a lot, there had to be a certain amount of integrity that went into the decision or perhaps the natural growth of a young and virile man into what he had become, still virile, but more mature now.

"You like that?" he asked.

"What grown woman wouldn't?"

He kissed her again, nothing too invasive, just a warm touch to let her know how much she moved him.

When he leaned back, he saw her eyes had heated and was sure his had, as well. They shared a long look, Kendall tipping her head back slightly as she took in every detail of his face. Then she closed the distance between them, pressing her mouth to his.

Decker instantly responded, his pulse jumping and

every male nerve in him coming to attention. He kissed her firmer, seeking more and getting it. Kendall parted her lips and he tasted her longingly. He lifted her so she straddled him and she looped her arms around his neck. The feel of her nakedness intimately against him heated his blood.

Voices alerted him to the danger of being caught like this. Kendall moved off him, wiping hair away from her face, looking flushed and breathless.

Laughter and soft talking indicated another couple had found the trail. He heard something move in the trees nearby. Was the couple trying to sneak to the spring unseen?

Decker splashed the spring water. The couple stopped making any sound and then the man said, "Someone's already there."

"I know another place," the woman said and then they left.

"We better go back inside," Kendall said.

He wondered if the kiss had crowded her too much or if fear of discovery compelled her. She climbed out and took a towel while he stayed behind a moment to admire her nakedness before climbing out himself.

They dried off and dressed. By looking at them, no one would know they'd skinny-dipped in the spring. He might have a wrinkle or two more than when he arrived but not easily detectable. And Kendall looked amazing in that dress. She slipped on her heels and he took her hand as they headed back up the path.

As they reached the area where the couple had approached, Decker heard someone come up behind them.

Before he could react, that person slammed something hard against his head. He went down, feeling himself black out for a moment and then dizzily come to. He felt the back of his head and his hand came away bloody. He wasn't bleeding profusely but he'd been struck hard enough to break skin.

Next, he became aware of Kendall screaming and heard the sounds of her struggle. Whoever had hit him was attacking her! Decker staggered to his feet and started toward her screams. Around a curve in the path, he spotted a man attempting to abduct her. He held a two-inch-diameter log and raised it to hit her. She blocked the log with her forearms and twisted away, but the man tripped her, dropping the log. He started to bend to pick it up but Kendall crawled to her feet and started to run. The guy caught her just as Decker began gaining ground on them. The man held her around the waist and dragged her kicking and screaming into the trees.

Decker entered the trees behind them.

Busy with trying to control Kendall, the attacker didn't see Decker. When the man punched Kendall on her jaw, a wave of red-hot fury boiled up inside Decker. He grabbed a hold of the fellow's jacket and threw him backward and off Kendall. Kendall fell to her rear, looking dazed.

The man scrambled to his feet and charged Decker, who ducked out of the way of a punch and then gave the stranger a hard uppercut. The man stumbled back. Decker checked on Kendall, who sat holding her jaw.

"Are you all right?"

She nodded and Decker bolted after the man, fully intending on giving the guy a beating.

The stranger glanced back and saw him, eyes growing wider.

Decker chased him. He was fast, sprinting and dodging trees until he reached the parking area of The Chateau. The man got into a gray Toyota sedan and backed out of a parking space. Decker searched for his McLaren. It was a row over and down a few cars. He had a spare key and used it to get in, seeing the Toyota leaving the parking lot.

If Decker could catch up to him, the guy would not be able to escape him. The McLaren was a fast car, but the stranger had a head start.

Decker swung out onto the road and didn't see the Toyota. He knew which direction the driver went, so he sped up the McLaren and passed two cars before cresting a hill and finally spotting the other vehicle. The Toyota swerved around slow-moving van, then the driver lost control and crashed into a ditch.

Decker screeched the McLaren to a stop, seeing the stranger get out of his car and make another run for it.

He chased him, seeing him disappear into the woods. When Decker reached the edge, he found footprints in the snow and followed those. A few minutes later he came to a river, where the prints ended. He had no way of knowing which direction the attacker had gone.

He wanted to keep looking, but he recalled how the man had hit Kendall and how she'd looked so dazed. He had to get back to her to make sure she was really all right as she had claimed.

Getting into his car, he drove back to the parking lot and ran through the trees to where a crowd had gathered around Kendall.

"Excuse me. Let me through." He plowed through four people as gently as he could until he reached Kendall. She sat on a fallen log, looking up at Russ, who had his hand on her shoulder.

"I'm all right," Kendall said, then she saw Decker.

"Are you sure?" Decker crouched before her and took her hands in his. "You were hit pretty hard on the head."

"Yes." Kendall touched where the log had struck her. "I'm going to have a bump but really, I'm fine."

"I think we should take you to the hospital just in case."

"No, that's not necessary."

"You might not know how severe it is," Decker insisted. He wanted to be sure. "Let's get you checked."

He stood and compelled her to do the same. When she swayed a little, he became even more convinced she needed to go to the emergency room.

"Okay," she said. "I am a little dizzy."

"Maybe we should wait for the ambulance," one of the people in the crowd said.

"No," Kendall said, sounding adamant. "Decker?"

"I'll get her there."

Decker felt a little like a superhero. He got her safely to his car, belted her in and assured that she wasn't too unsteady. Her injuries weren't life-threatening but if left untreated could possibly become that. He'd heard stories. People ran into trees, bonked themselves on the head and a day later, boom, hemorrhage and death.

Now that he had found a woman he truly wanted to spend the rest of his life with, he wasn't about to let any harm—or any more harm—come her way.

Chapter 7

Kendall hadn't expected Decker to turn into a super-hero, but he had. He had no training in self-defense that she knew of. He was a businessman. But he'd fought off and chased her assailant as though he had been doing that all his life. The doctors had checked her out. She was fine, just as she'd known and had only gone to the hospital for Decker's sake. Ironically, his knock on the head had actually been worse than hers. He'd gotten a couple of stitches.

Now they had been released and he took her to his house. Kendall hadn't protested. She did not want to be alone after what happened. And her awe of Decker had added fuel to her attraction. She could take his hand and led him to the nearest bedrooom right now.

"Dad said Trey and his deputy will be by to talk to

us," Decker said as he let her into his house. "In the morning."

Sheriff Trey Colton was Decker's cousin. "Okay." She was glad she wouldn't have to talk to anyone tonight.

"The car the assailant abandoned after he crashed into the ditch was traced to a stolen vehicle in the county."

Walking into the entry, Kendall took in Decker's open and large house. "All this for just one person?"

"I plan on having kids," he said.

They'd sort of talked about that already. She wanted kids as well, but that was such a big step with a man she hardly knew.

She went into the living room, taking in the exposed beams above and a big gabled window where during the day she'd expect to see a great view. A console table ran along the back of a chocolate-brown sofa which faced a light-colored stone fireplace and two chairs that matched the sofa. An oversize square coffee table was full of books. She moved closer to read some of the titles. Many were travel books. The ceramic bowl with stone balls inside was a surprising decorative touch to an otherwise masculine and earthy room. Masculine, like Decker.

She looked at him, admiring his muscular body, his height and handsome face that had grown stubble through the day.

"Do you want some tea before we try to get some sleep?" Decker asked, catching her looking at him.

It was getting late but she doubted she'd be able to

sleep after the events of the evening. "That sounds good."

He continued to stare at her and she had no desire to look away.

Finally he turned with a slight grin.

She followed him into the kitchen, another spacious and beautiful room. Brown, black and cream-colored granite-topped counters lined two and a quarter of the walls with an island in the middle. A dining area was in a turreted space and the island could seat six.

"How many kids are you planning to have?" she asked.

"As many as you want."

She eyed him. She'd rather not turn into a baby-making machine. "One maybe two."

"Okay."

His easy agreement told her he would be a flexible partner in their marriage. She liked how considerate he was. She liked even more what they would have to do to procreate. Warming too much, she wandered to the windows in the turret. Outdoor lights illuminated the dormant landscape and the edge of pine trees.

"Do you think that man attacked you at random?" Decker asked as he started water boiling.

She turned to face him. "I've been going over that in my mind. I can't think of anyone else who'd stalk me and then try to kidnap me."

"It doesn't make any sense."

"To me, either. I have no enemies." She walked back into the kitchen, where Decker put tea bags in two cups.

"No old boyfriends who might have a vendetta against you?" he asked.

"I've never seen that man until that day my mother and I came out of the bridal shop." Kendall was friendly to everyone she met, and most of the men she'd had long relationships with had broken up with her, including Gabe, when he had cheated. The one man she had broken up with who had been hurt by it was a mild-mannered man, an engineer for an aerospace company. Last she had heard he'd married and had two kids and lived in Texas.

"Then it must be some random quack who saw you and took a perverse interest in you."

Kendall rubbed her arms. "Yeah."

"Kendall, I want you to move in with me," he said.

When she was about to protest he said, "You can sleep in a separate bedroom if it makes you more comfortable. You'll be safe here. I'll keep you safe."

She did think he had a valid point, and he had proved himself more than capable of protecting her. But Kendall wasn't a weak woman. She may still be a bit shaken after nearly being kidnapped, but by tomorrow she'd be back to herself.

Also, she may talk about getting married and agree to help in getting invitations sent, but something inside her still hedged. She didn't have to wonder why, either. Why on earth had she even considered marrying Decker Colton in less than a month?

"I'll take you to get your things tomorrow, after we talk to the deputy," he said.

She angled her head, still uncertain.

"Just give it a try, okay? You can always leave if I scare you too much." He sounded serious.

Now she smiled. He had a deadpan way about him but some of the things he said were funny. And he could be very persuasive.

"All right."

"Finally." He slipped his arm around her waist and drew her closer for a kiss.

He must have intended for that to be a quick one, but he heated Kendall up even more and she tilted her head for another. He kissed her again and she slid her hands up his arms to his shoulders. Decker pressed harder and she opened her mouth. Stabbing pain from where she had been hit made her whimper softly and move back.

"Sorry," Decker said.

"I'm okay." She smiled wryly. "I got a little carried away. You're heroics really turned me on."

"Remind me to be heroic more often. As long as it doesn't involve you getting hurt."

He poured hot water in the cups and she took one, bobbing the bag a few times and wondering yet again if she was about to make the biggest mistake of her life. Her body seemed headed that way, as much as she wanted Decker right now.

The next morning, Daria Bloom looked fit in her light brown sheriff deputy uniform. She held a small notebook and a mechanical pencil and finished jotting down Kendall's description of the stranger who had nearly abducted her. A strikingly attractive Caucasian/African American woman with smooth medium-brown skin, sparkling golden brown eyes and short dark hair, she was smart as a whip with a no-nonsense attitude that served her well in her line of work.

Trey had started out the questioning but now let Daria have a turn. He had nearly the same skin tone as she did and close-cropped dark hair. He also wore a cowboy hat.

"Could Kendall's attacker be the same man who killed Bianca Rouge?" Decker asked.

Why had he asked such a question? She supposed because of the randomness of her attack.

"I'm not sure if this is related to her murder and April Thomas's disappearance, but the fact that your attacker tried to abduct you has me wondering," Daria said. "April looks a lot like the Rouge victim. Both are young, thin, with dark hair and dark eyes." She studied Kendall. "You might have some resemblance but not enough to sway me a hundred percent. You have blond hair and blue eyes."

Maybe looks didn't matter. The missing woman had no connection to Bianca that Kendall was aware of. Kendall had no connection to them either, which made the random-stalker-and-attacker theory more credible.

"This is a new description of the man if it is related," Trey said. "And probably the most detailed."

That was something. "I'd feel so much better if you could find and catch him." Kendall didn't want to fear being the target of a potential serial kidnapper and killer.

"We're definitely working on it. Don't be afraid. I am not convinced your case is related to Bianca's and

April's. I'm not even convinced April's disappearance is related to the Rouge murder."

Not knowing was more dangerous than knowing, wasn't it? For Kendall it was. No one knew who killed Bianca Rouge and no one knew who had kidnapped April—if she'd even been kidnapped. Without a body it was difficult to say.

"What if someone has it out for the Coltons?" Decker asked.

Kendall gaped at him. Why would anyone have it out for his family? And if so, who? The less fortunate? Someone wronged in a business deal? She supposed it was possible, but why go after her? To get to Decker? Russ? It had been his dad's idea to get them married after all.

"Anything's possible at this point," Trey said. "We don't have much to go on. There wasn't anything found at the near-abduction scene and nothing in the car, not even prints or anything we can use for DNA testing. We've got people working on the stolen car, trying to find out who could have taken it but nothing concrete so far."

Her attacker could have been anyone. The reason would not be known until after they discovered who the man was. What if they never did?

Later that afternoon, Kendall had everything she needed in Decker's car and stopped by her parents' house. She'd called her mother this morning to tell her what happened and her mother insisted on seeing her.

Decker's cell phone rang and he stayed in the foyer to take the call.

Kendall's mother hugged her. "I'm so glad you're all right, sweetie."

Behind her, Bernard looked grim.

"Why would anyone try to kidnap you?" her father demanded.

"Sheriff Colton and Deputy Sheriff Bloom think it could be random or someone out to get the Coltons."

"Random?" Her mother turned to glance back at her father, who barely paid her any attention.

Kendall began to get a strange feeling. Her parents were acting awfully skittish. She could see how they'd be concerned about her and what had nearly happened to her, but they could see she was all right. Shouldn't they be more relieved than nervous?

"The sheriff and his deputy think it is," Bernard said.

Marion eyed him with pursed lips. "It's only one possibility."

"They also think it could be someone after the Coltons," her father argued.

"Yes, and that is also only one possibility."

Meaning there were others?

"You yourself said you heard people talking in town about why such a nice woman like Kendall would marry a scoundrel like Decker Colton," her dad said to Marion.

People were talking that way about her? Was Decker a scoundrel? Why did they say that about him?

"There's another, more viable possibility," Marion said.

"Marion…"

What in the world was going on here?

"Tell her, Bernard," Marion said. "Moreover, we should tell Trey and Daria."

"No." Her father flat-out denied that suggestion.

Kendall looked from her mom to her dad and back to Marion again. "Tell me what? And why wouldn't you go to the sheriff if you know something?"

"It might be random," her father insisted.

"Damn it, Bernard. I'm not going to play this game anymore. Your daughter was almost kidnapped!"

"What is going on?" Kendall demanded. She glanced back to see Decker still on the phone, looking focused and not paying any attention to what was happening in the living room.

"It might be someone out to get the Coltons," Bernard said. "They have a lot of enemies in this town."

"I don't think anyone would target me to get at Decker." She supposed it was possible but it felt more random.

"Hadley Forestry is in financial trouble, Kendall," her mother said. "Your near abduction might be some kind of warning."

"It's temporary trouble. Nothing you need to worry about," her father interjected.

"What kind of financial trouble?" Kendall asked.

Is that why her father had pushed so hard for her to marry Decker? She began to get angry as she awaited an explanation.

"We're nearly bankrupt," Marion said.

Bernard let out a heavy breath and rubbed his eyes. "Marion, you worry too much."

"Your father and I have refinanced the house and borrowed more than we can pay back right now. It won't be long before we're forcibly removed from the property and our business doors shut for good." Her eyes moistened with the near onslaught of tears.

"Why didn't you tell me?" Kendall asked, looking at her father.

He reluctantly met her eyes.

"Go on," Marion said, sounding disgusted with him. "Tell her."

"I thought I could find a way out," he said.

"By getting me to marry Decker?" She glanced back at Decker and saw him still talking into this phone. What would he think of all this?

"It wasn't my idea. Russ approached me about it."

"And it never crossed your mind that my marrying Decker would solve your financial troubles?" Kendall asked.

"I can't say it never crossed my mind," he admitted. "I would have never asked you to do that to save our company, Kendall."

She believed him, which softened the sting a little. "Is that why you asked me to come to work for you?" she asked.

"Yes. And you have helped some. It's just not enough soon enough to make a difference," her father said wearily. "I'm talking to some investors and planning on a reorganization that will include some layoffs, but I'm not sure if it will work out."

"It won't," Marion said. "We're going to lose everything."

Her mother could be a bit of a drama queen at times. Kendall would help her father figure out a way to resolve the financial issues.

"What about my trust?" she asked.

"No. You are not giving us your trust money," Marion retorted.

"It wouldn't be enough anyway," Bernard said.

That meant the company was tens of millions in the red, probably in the upper tens of millions.

"I can't believe you didn't tell me!" Kendall cried. "You should have told me as soon as Russ came to you with the idea of me and Decker marrying."

"I feel terrible about that, Kendall. But I can't lie. Your marriage to Decker will save us."

He assumed she'd bail him out as soon as she did marry him. As Kendall thought that over, she realized she would. She could not stand back and watch her parents lose everything. But neither could she marry in deception like that.

Looking at Decker again, she saw he'd finished his call. Should she tell him?

"Don't say anything yet, Kendall," her father pleaded. "Please."

He was worried that Decker wouldn't want to marry her if he learned her family didn't have the money he thought they did.

That riled her but she also wasn't sure herself. Would Decker think less of her knowing she wasn't worth what he and his father assumed?

"Everything all right?" Decker asked, looking at her and then her parents.

"They're just worried about me," Kendall said.

Decker nodded as Kendall saw the relief in her father's eyes. She wasn't going to tell anyone. Not yet.

"You don't have to worry." Decker put his arm around her. "I won't let anything happen to her."

"He did chase off my attacker," Kendall said.

"Then you'll be safer with him," Marion murmured. "I don't want you by yourself in your house."

Kendall didn't say the reason why her mother didn't want her to be alone. Someone Hadley Forestry owed money to might be attempting to kidnap her for ransom.

"I've got to stop by The Lodge. Something's come up I need to take care of," Decker said. "Can you come with me?"

It was after five and she was getting hungry, having skipped lunch to pack.

"Yes, she can," Bernard said.

Kendall sent him a warning look. Was he still pushing her to marry Decker?

"She can take as much time off as she needs. In fact, don't plan on coming back to work until after the wedding."

Kendall saw that Decker noticed her distraction. She was quiet and kept staring out the passenger window.

"Are you all right?" he asked.

She turned to him with a small smile. "Yes. Just thinking about my parents. They're so worried."

"You'll be fine. And so will they. Just call them every day."

He seemed so certain. He also didn't know someone might be after her to force her father to pay money owed? Money he didn't have.

The snow had gotten heavier, the kind of storm with giant flakes. While beautiful, the roads were turning slick and visibility had decreased dramatically in just the last five minutes.

Decker turned onto the road leading to The Lodge. "We might have a tough time getting back to my house later," he said.

"Oh, darn, then we'd have to stay in one of those nice rooms." It felt good to lighten the mood—and get her mind off her parents' deception.

"I have a suite at The Lodge. I stay there a lot," he said.

They entered the posh lodge. This was the first Kendall had seen of the interior and it was far richer than she imagined. White marble floors and glittering chandeliers offset the touch of rugged with exposed wood beams and a giant rock fireplace. Two clerks stood behind the lighted golden front of the reception desk.

A man waited at the end, watching their approach. In a snug gray suit with a white shirt and a banded black-and-gray tie, he definitely liked fashion. His ankles were visible beneath the hem of the slacks and his short sandy-blond hair was neatly styled.

"Mr. Colton," he said as they reached the desk.

"This is Seth Harris, my front desk manager," Decker said to Kendall.

"Kendall Hadley." She shook his hand.

"Kendall is going to be staying with me so you'll likely see her around The Lodge on occasion."

"Yes, I know who you are," Seth said to her. "And congratulations."

He referred to the wedding, of course. Fleetingly she wondered what he thought about that, whether he believed rumors.

Seth turned to Decker. "Molly Gilford should be here any moment."

Just as he said that a woman of average height with a blond bob and a black business skirt and jacket appeared.

Decker must have spoken with Molly on the phone earlier and he'd come here to deal with some sort of issue.

"Thanks for stopping by," Molly said. "The guest is insisting on talking with you."

"No problem. What room is he in?"

"The Primrose Penthouse."

"I've spoken with him as well," Seth said. "I think he's much calmer now."

"Thanks, Seth." Decker put his hand on Kendall's lower back and they headed for the elevators.

"What happened?"

"A famous news anchor frequently stays here and is always hard to please. Apparently his eggs were cooked too well and he isn't happy with the slow response."

"Oh, boo hoo."

He grinned as they entered the elevator. "Seth is a smooth talker with the guests. He's good at his job."

"Handy."

At the top floor they exited and walked to the door with Primrose printed on a gold plaque.

Decker knocked and a few seconds later a clean-cut

fiftyish man with short gray hair and deceptively mild brown eyes answered.

"Decker Colton," he said in way of introduction. "I'm sorry to hear your breakfast wasn't what you ordered?"

"It took them an hour to bring me up the right order," he said, annoyed.

"Tomorrow's breakfast will be on us to make up for that."

"It's a little late for that. Today's breakfast was ruined because of your staff's incompetence."

"I'll speak to them immediately. It won't happen again."

"You should hire the right people. People who take pride in their jobs and who don't make mistakes. I expect nothing less from a five-star resort like this."

"I expect nothing less than that as well, sir. I can assure you I won't let it go lightly."

The man seemed to soften. He glanced at Kendall. "Is she the one who made the eggs?"

"No, this is my fiancée, Kendall Hadley."

"Oh." The man appeared to check himself. "My apologies, ma'am. I meant no disrespect."

"None taken," she replied, thinking this man could look on the brighter side of things much more often then he likely did. She recognized him from the morning news program she sometimes watched. Now that she knew his true nature, she wouldn't ever watch it again.

Decker jotted down his cell number and handed it to the man. "Call me in the morning with your breakfast order and I'll see to it personally that it's done exactly right."

The man nodded, clearly pacified that he'd gotten his way and forced everyone to kiss up. "Thank you."

"Of course. Good day." With that Decker walked with Kendall down the hall.

"How often do you have to do that?" she asked.

"Not often. Most people who come here are happy and enjoy the many amenities."

"I would hate dealing with the sourpusses," she said.

"I humor them. I know what kind of people they are. It doesn't bother me." He stopped her from going into the elevator. "Let's go down here."

She walked with him to a double door at the end of the hall. Using a card key, he unlocked the door and held it for her.

"What are you doing?" she asked, entering the room.

"This is my suite."

He flipped on a light to reveal an elegant room. A lamp was on a console behind one couch, another couch on the other side of a coffee table. Beyond that floor-to-ceiling windows took up the entire opposite wall with a balcony on the other side, two doors on each end providing access. There was a table with four leather chairs before the windows, a nice place to gather for cocktails.

snow fall. Decker came to stand beside her.

"Beautiful isn't it?" he asked huskily.

Was he referring to this spectacular room or the snow?

"Yes, everything."

He wrapped his arms around her from behind, putting his head beside hers as they watched it snow.

Flutters of warmth tickled her abdomen.

"When we remodeled I hired a really good interior decorator," he said.

Kendall heard the pride in his tone and eased away from him so she could face him. She knew he had humility but something about wealth and material things pleased him.

"What draws you to this?" She raised her palms to the interior of this splendid suite and then stretched a hand to the massive windows.

Need she say more?

At first he just looked at her with an impassive gaze she had begun to recognize. He was a cool cookie most of the time, but when business opportunities presented themselves, he was aggressive.

Several seconds passed. He took his time, looking through the windows at the snow and more.

At last he turned from the window. The light in his eyes changed, more revealing now, more emotional. She couldn't tell what he felt, though.

"It's not what you think," he finally said.

What did he mean by that? "I don't understand."

He turned to the window, to the thick and windless fall of snow.

"The mountains," he said. "The geology. When I was a kid, growing up, that's what fascinated me."

He spoke from the heart—again. Kendall struggled with falling further in love with him. No—further infatuated with him. She would not call it love. Her high school crush could not have that much of an impact on how she felt, could it?

"Before my father expanded, the lodge was natural. Historical."

He sparked more curiosity. "You would have preferred it that way? Untouched?"

"No." He faced her directly, with the slight shake of his head. "It was me who turned this resort into what it is today. My father had a vision. I made it a reality."

What she'd say next would probably hurt him. "But it was his vision."

As she anticipated, Decker turned away.

"Don't you think I know that?" he shot back.

"Yes, of course, but you live *his* vision, not your own." How did he feel about that?

"This resort is as much mine as his." He glanced at her, clearly not happy with what she insinuated, that he followed in his father's shadow.

He did have his own input into making The Lodge into a grand palace, but he had followed his father and was still following. Deep down she suspected he knew that all too well and likely wrestled with it often.

"I feel that way about my father," she admitted. "Not exactly the same, but I came back here because he asked me to."

She averted her head because now she knew why he had asked her to come back. He needed help saving his company.

Chapter 8

The snowstorm had picked up, now blowing and drifting. Decker had gotten two calls from his staff saying guests couldn't make the drive to the lodge. He'd sent someone to go pick them up. Now she sat with him on the chairs around the cocktail table, finishing up a conversation about when they were kids. The only light came from the gas fireplace and the balcony lights that illuminated the heavily falling snow.

She told him about the time her parents had taken her to the annual Mountain Fair, held at the end of each summer. Local artists had booths and vendors offered food of all kinds. There was always live entertainment, as well. She remembered seeing him there with his family. In the eleventh grade, he'd had a girl with him, of course.

He felt a pang of regret because he didn't remember

seeing her there. He did remember the girl, though. She'd been the one he had broken up with after high school.

"I had such a crush on you back then," Kendall confessed, still reminiscing. "All through my senior year."

"Not anymore?" he teased.

She smiled and said nothing, just sipped some wine and put the glass on the table.

On impulse, Decker stood and held out his hand. He had some light jazz playing.

She gave him her hand and stood. He led her to the open space between the cocktail table and the seating area and drew her closer.

She put her hand on his shoulder, leaving her other in his hand as he moved her into a slow rhythm.

"Is that why you're going to marry me?" he asked. "Do you still have a crush on me?"

"Like I've told you before, I was curious."

"Well, has the crush returned?"

"Wouldn't you love to know." The light in her smiling eyes arrested him for a few seconds.

"You might as well tell me. We're going to be married in a little more than two weeks."

"I could back out before then."

Hearing her mischievous tone, he took heart that she intended to go through with this.

"Once word gets around you're on board with the wedding, my dad will be happy."

"Good, then maybe our parents will leave us alone," she said, sliding her arms up to enfold his neck.

The action sent fire coiling inside him. She fit him

so well. A tall woman, her head came to just below his, tipped up now with a dreamy look.

He didn't attempt to stop his reaction. He just kissed her, soft at first, as their bodies continued to sway together in a slow dance.

She touched the side of his face, then gradually angled her head and urged him for more.

Already embracing her, he indulged the instinct to cup her rear with both hands and then feel her curves from her waist to her breasts. She moved her hand to his shoulder and drew back from the long, heated kiss.

He saw her eyes looking up at him, glazed over with passion. He felt the same. This thing between them had sprung from seemingly nothing, a spark that had no explanation except that perhaps it had lain dormant ever since high school. He had always thought she was pretty. He just had never had the chance to get to know her. Funny, how one dinner had changed all that.

Taking her hand, he led her to the bedroom, a spacious room with a king bed and more floor-to-ceiling windows. It also had access to the deck.

She began to undress so he took her lead and did the same, enjoying her fluid movements as she neatly draped her clothes on the chair beside the bed. She crawled under the covers and he joined her.

Not wanting to rush, he drew her into his arms and she snuggled up against him. He rested his head against hers and watched it snow with her for a while, the warmth of their attraction simmering, waiting to ignite into more. Snow pattered against the glass and blew in thick bands in the exterior light, but they were cozy in here.

Reaching for a remote, he turned on the gas fireplace and then rolled to his side to caress Kendall's head, meeting her eyes before kissing her. He took his time before moving on top of her. She made room for him, inexplicable desire taking flight. Hearing and feeling her breath, he knew she experienced the same.

He entered her slowly, wanting this to mean something. He didn't stop and ponder why or what he wanted it to mean. He only acted on instinct and the magic the two of them created.

Moving back and forth, it didn't take long for either of them to reach a peak. He couldn't resist moving faster, going deeper, loving how she arched and made a sultry sound as she came.

After lying on her a few moments while they caught their breath and returned to the tangible world, he at last rolled off her. With her curled beside him, he couldn't remember ever feeling better. Things were going his way. He'd be married to a wonderful woman. They'd start a family. This was exactly what he wanted, what he was missing in his life.

"How do you feel?" he asked tenderly.

Lifting her head, pausing in drawing circles on his chest with her forefinger, she looked at him. "You have to ask?"

"Good, I know, but about all of this."

She rested her head on his shoulder again, resuming her drawing. After a while, she finally said, "Good," in a quiet but lighthearted tone.

He kissed her forehead and chuckled. "Me too."

She stopped drawing and he saw her eyes had closed, content and comfortable.

"Our parents will be really happy," he said. "My dad, for one, will love to hear how well things are going between us."

Kendall said nothing and after a few moments she moved away from him to lie on her back. He saw her staring up at the ceiling, seeming to be deep in some somber thought.

"What's the matter?"

She glanced at him and gave him a slight lift of her mouth in what she might intend as a smile but he sensed something troubling her.

"Darling, what is it?" He rolled to his side, propping his head on his hand.

"Nothing."

"Yes…it's something. Tell me."

After a bit she shook her head on the pillow. "Just nervous I guess."

About the wedding? He could buy that but he didn't think that was all. She'd acted the same way on the way here.

"What did you and your parents talk about when I was on the phone?" he asked.

"Not much."

"It seemed lengthy." And like more than a casual talk. He'd felt the tension when he'd come into the room.

"They keep badgering me about the nuptials, asking me how things are going. That sort of thing."

"Oh." He leaned over and kissed her. "Tell them about tonight then. That will get them to stop."

She swatted him with her pillow. "I'm not telling them anything about tonight."

He chuckled. Of course they wouldn't talk about the intimacy. He only meant the perfect match, a great business deal—one with benefits.

A few days later, Kendall waited at the highway pull-off where she and Decker had parked for their hike. She had fallen into a sort of domestic routine. She and Decker spent their days working—much to her father's protest until she convinced him Decker had to work and she'd be twiddling her thumbs all day. Then she and Decker spent their evenings together, having dinner prepared for them at home and giving each other debriefs of their day at work, winding down for nighttime and sleeping together. She couldn't keep her hands off him.

She saw no sign of the man who'd attacked her and had begun to think maybe he'd been scared off.

Today she had a planned trip to go check on her wolves. She had spoken to the US Fish and Wildlife Service on numerous occasions and at last they had assigned a wildlife biologist who would accompany her. If they saw the wolves that would make this an official gray wolf sighting. There had been a few other unofficial sightings, where hikers or others had spotted a gray wolf but no one in an official capacity had been able to verify it.

Since someone else was going with her, Decker had only put up a small fuss. He didn't like her going anywhere he didn't think she was safe. His big house had ample security, but he worried about her even going to work.

"You're not going to be one of those overly possessive men, are you?" she had asked him.

"No. I just don't want anything to happen to you."

"You can't watch me twenty-four-seven, so how about a little faith in me, okay?"

And with that he'd backed off.

Seeing a truck approach, she saw the US Fish and Wildlife emblem on the passenger door and watched the truck slow, the blinker going on. The driver parked behind her Land Rover. She stood near the trailhead, ready and waiting with her backpack. Today was overcast so she'd dressed and packed accordingly. The biologist's name was Ben Kennedy. He got out, a big man who looked in his early forties. He retrieved his pack and strode toward her. She already felt safe. Her stalker would be a fool to try anything with this man next to her.

"Sorry I'm late," Ben said as he came to a stop. "Traffic was terrible leaving Lakewood."

"No problem." He must have left very early to make it here by this time of morning—after nine now.

"Let's get going." She started for the hiking trail.

Ben made small talk. They exchanged details about their careers and he asked her about how she'd found this wolf pack.

"If we can confirm their location, this is going to mean a lot to us," he said.

He didn't tell her anything she didn't already know.

"We know the wolves have migrated down from Montana and Wyoming and are starting to show a strong presence in northern Colorado, but marking them this far south will be remarkable."

She turned a little and nodded.

"Really. Our office is going to be indebted to you for this find."

"I'm just doing what I love."

"We are too, so I'm sure you understand how significant a gray wolf pack near Roaring Springs will be."

"Is," she said. "They're here and established." She had to admit, having to go through this formal "confirmation" of her find annoyed her. She had a solid reputation. Why couldn't they consider her word good enough? She could send photos.

"I believe you. Sorry for the necessity to prove it. Call it bureaucracy. Tell me more about the pack."

She went through what she'd told Decker, adding, "The mated pair really seem bonded. I've seen them close, touching noses and sniffing each other. And the way they watch their offspring. It's like our own families only they have a different way of communicating."

"Yeah. Wolves are my favorite to study. That's why they sent me."

Kendall was glad they'd sent the best.

"Are you married?" he asked after a while.

Uncomfortable that he might be checking to see if she was available, she said, "I'm living with someone at the moment."

"He must not be a weak-kneed man if he's with you."

"He's not." She didn't say more. They reached the point where they had to veer off the trail and she took him the distance to the last location she and Decker had seen them. This time they weren't there.

"We have to be careful, but I know where their den is."

They hiked the distance and crouched low and hidden. Kendall heard the wolves before she saw them.

"Wow," Ben whispered. "That is incredible."

The mated pair had their heads turned in their direction, indicating they had heard their approach. Right now they were another animal to them, and they did not seem threatened. In fact, this pair didn't seem to scare easily, which was probably why they would continue to be a healthy pack. A strong pack.

"Let's go," Ben said. "We'll take it from here. I'll study them and put a tracker on one. We'll keep in touch to let you know status. And on behalf of everyone with the Fish and Wildlife Service, we thank you."

She looked one last time at the wolves, sorry that she wouldn't see them again. But Ben was right. He had the experience to track them. She followed him down the mountain, her thoughts turning to the upcoming evening with Decker.

Later that day, Kendall had parted ways with the wildlife biologist and had driven to her house to pick up a few more things she needed. She left there and headed toward Decker's house.

She drove perhaps ten minutes before she noticed a car behind her. She knew she hadn't been followed to the trailhead, but it was possible her stalker had waited somewhere hidden near her house. She was close to the turn to Decker's. This car was different than the other one she'd seen the stalker in.

She really had no choice other than to make the turn to Decker's. Her heart rate leapt into a faster pace.

She could drive to the police station, but what if the man decided to try and run her off the mountain route? She stepped on the gas on the road toward Decker's driveway.

The car behind her sped up too.

It was him.

"Oh, no," she breathed, feeling the blood drain from her face.

She drove as fast as she could on the winding road, but the man behind her was a good driver and had a V-8. She drove a V-6.

He caught up to her, so close she couldn't see the front of the car.

Her heart raced.

Exactly what she feared. He'd try to run her off the road in an attempt to abduct her.

She swerved into the next turn. She could see Decker's driveway.

"Please have the stupid gate open," she said out loud.

She had called him when she left her house, so he knew she was on her way.

Closer and closer she came to the driveway. She held her breath.

Seeing the gate was open, she let out a gush of air in relief. She swung into the turn, hitting the metal edge of the gate. Her stalker would be on camera now if he followed.

She looked behind her.

The car drove past the driveway. Stopping in front of Decker's house, she got out and hurried to the door, glancing back just to be sure no one had followed. Thankfully, no one had.

She entered and closed the door, locking it and resting her head against the hard surface.

Hearing someone come up beside her, she jumped and turned to see Decker. He reached to press some buttons on the control box beside the door. He closed the gate and set the alarm.

"What happened?" he asked, his brow furrowing with concern.

She moved to press herself against him, safe at last.

He held her and rubbed her back. "Hey."

She leaned back and looked up at him. "He followed me again, almost ran me off the road."

Decker's jaw flexed, revealing his anger. "I should have been with you."

"You can't always be my hero," she said, smiling shakily.

Stepping back, she went into the living room and put her purse onto a chair.

He went with her, standing just outside the seating area. "No more driving yourself. You go with one of my drivers."

"No argument from me on that."

"Was it the same man?" he asked.

"I didn't see him. It was a different car."

He stopped as she faced him, putting his hands on his hips with a concerned dip to his brow. "That's not good." He looked at her. "This isn't random, Kendall. Someone is targeting you. The question is, why?"

Kendall was afraid she already knew. Who had her father borrowed money from who would go to such extremes to get it back? How desperate had her father become?

"Are you sure there isn't anyone who might want to do you harm?"

"Me? No." At least she could answer that honestly—kind of. She didn't have any enemies, but her father must.

He walked to her and put his hands on her upper arms. "We'll have to be careful until we can determine who is after you and why."

She only nodded. Oh, she'd be careful all right. And she'd welcome Decker's security measures.

He lowered his hands and went to the telephone, from which he called Trey. Kendall listened to his side of the conversation and got as much as the fact that Trey would put the word out to look for the car that had chased her. When he hung up, he came back to her and took her into his arms. She rested her hands on his chest.

Looking up at him, her heart did a little flop. His dark eyes radiated so much warmth and tenderness, and yet he had a rugged edge to him as well, a silent but unmistakable aura of confidence.

He was everything she'd ever dreamed of finding in a man. Maybe more. Which alarmed her.

Would he always be just about business? He'd claimed to want a family. That didn't jive with someone who devoted life to only business.

She had to know what she was getting herself into. "Decker, can I ask you a very personal question?"

"Sure. Don't be afraid to ask me anything."

He might be able to handle it but would he answer her honestly?

"Do you think you can ever fall in love?" she asked.

A hard mask came over his face. He took several seconds before he asked, "Can I?"

"Or do you think it's at all possible?" she clarified.

Again he took several seconds before he answered.

"I think it's possible to fall in love, but I don't think it will ever happen to me."

Was he being overly pessimistic or did he really believe he'd never fall in love? And if he believed he'd never fall in love, then he must not think he'd ever fall in love with *her*.

"What if I fall in love with you?" she whispered.

"Then you'll be safe with me, Kendall. I would never hurt you. I want this to last our lifetime."

She supposed she should be glad to hear that, but instead she felt incredibly disappointed.

He dipped his head, clearly recognizing her reaction. "Hey. If the impossible were to happen, then there isn't any other woman I'd rather fall in love with than you."

Again, she supposed she should be happy to hear that but it only intensified her inner turmoil.

"I'm tired. I'm going to run a bath and go to bed early." She disentangled herself from his grip and went around the sofa to avoid passing too close to him.

As she walked away, he called after her, "Kendall."

"It's all right, Decker. I just need to be alone tonight."

He let her go and she was relieved. She wasn't prepared for how sad that brief talk had made her. Maybe she should tell him about her father's money troubles. Then maybe he'd end the engagement and find another business opportunity. She'd be spared what she was certain would turn out to be a major disaster for her. Because now she was sure she could fall madly in love with him.

Chapter 9

Decker hadn't slept well last night. Kendall's crest-fallen eyes were burned into his mind. He'd been honest with her but she obviously felt different. She believed she *could* fall in love. She believed she could fall in love with *him*. That made him feel uncomfortable. Would she end up like other women and demand too much from him?

Even as that thought came, he felt something refute that in his gut. Kendall would not end up like other women. She was uniquely special to him. Didn't she see that? They got along so well, in and out of bed. But maybe she had begun to want more from him.

Did that mean she had feelings for him? He had feelings for her too. They were great together. What was she so upset about?

His father burst into the office like he normally did, although this time the door banged against the stop.

"We need to talk," Russ said.

"Can't you ever knock?"

Russ just shut the office door and stalked toward the desk. "I just heard Bernard Hadley is on the brink of bankruptcy."

That came as a shock. Kendall's family had been extremely wealthy for as long as he had known her.

"Are you sure?" he asked.

"I just had it confirmed. He's past due on several bank notes."

Decker didn't ask how he had found that out. His dad had ways of finding information like that.

"So what's the issue?" Why was Russ so mad? His dad had originally thought a joining with the Hadleys would be smart financially, but it could still be a good move.

"What's the issue?" His dad's voice raised. "They don't have any money!"

"You didn't research that before you approached Bernard?" Decker knew that would grate on his father's nerves.

And it did. Russ's face turned red. "I didn't think I had to. That family was worth millions. What happened?"

"Have you asked him?"

"No I haven't asked him," Russ grew even more annoyed. "The wedding is off!"

Decker leaned back, surprised his dad would take it that far. "You want me to call off the wedding because

Kendall's dad is going through a rough patch? He'll bounce back."

"Yeah, on Colton money!" Russ leaned on Decker's desk, bringing his angry face closer. "That louse should have said something instead of throwing his daughter at us."

Decker was beginning to lose his patience. He stood. "You were the one who approached him, Dad."

Russ straightened. "So? He should have told me he was broke!"

"Why? Is this arrangement only for the two of you to prosper financially? Maybe Bernard thought Kendall would make a good match for me—beyond a business deal." As soon as he said it he realized he had been treating this as a business deal, but Kendall was more than that.

"Yes," Russ said, looking incredulous.

Decker walked around his desk. "Okay, first of all, I wouldn't marry a woman just to make you money." He stopped inches from his father. "She would have to be someone I felt I could live the rest of my life with whether I loved her or not. I wouldn't marry her if she weren't at least that."

He saw his father's surprise that Decker had gotten in his face.

"Second," Decker continued, "Kendall has a choice in this too. She wouldn't marry me if she didn't feel the same as me."

"Oh, really. She probably knew about Hadley Forestry's money problems before the two of you had that first dinner."

Decker hadn't thought of that. Had she known? Reflecting over all the times they'd shared together, all they'd talked about, he couldn't believe she'd do something that shady.

"She would have told me."

"Would she have?" his dad challenged. "Or would she put her family before a man she barely knows?"

He had a valid point. Decker had to take a few minutes to think that over. Deep down he did not believe Kendall would deceive him like that. Then again, she'd been acting strange lately. Last night, for example, when she had asked him about love. She'd seemed upset with the prospect of not having love in a marriage. Did she struggle with the notion of marrying to save her father's company?

"Call off the wedding," Russ said.

"I'll talk to her."

Russ's lips pursed in frustration before he said, "What good is talking going to do? The Hadleys are broke. We can't be associated with their kind."

"Broke people are human just like us, Dad. Do you have to be such an ass all the time?"

His dad's head drew back in disbelief. "Did you just talk to me like that?"

"You don't have to stick your nose up at people who aren't filthy stinking rich." Decker was so sick of his father's attitude.

"You better watch it, Decker. I can still put someone else in charge of The Lodge."

"Go ahead!" Decker roared back. "I'm tired of you constantly throwing that in my face! Go ahead and find someone else who will do a better job than me. Go ahead and hand over a piece of your precious empire to someone outside the family!"

For once his father was speechless. He just stared at Decker in shock.

"I did everything you wanted ever since I graduated from high school. I gave up any dreams of my own for you."

"What dreams?" Russ scoffed. "You always wanted to be part of this company."

"No, I didn't, Dad. I wanted to go to college for business, but I wanted to get into something other than serving the rich and snobby."

"What's gotten into you? Did that Hadley woman warp your brain?"

"She opened my mind to a lot of things," he said.

His dad pointed his finger at him. "You call off that wedding, son."

Or what? He'd fire him? For the first time in his life, he didn't give a rat's ass what his dad thought or what he'd do in retaliation.

"Whatever trouble the Hadleys are in, we can help them," Decker said. It would be good for his father to do something charitable for people he viewed as beneath him.

"Help them? With Colton money? Over my dead body!"

"Okay," Decker tossed over his shoulder as he left the office.

He had to find Kendall.

* * *

Kendall's father explained that the man in charge of inventory overestimated demand and that was what caused the downward spiral. He had fired the man, and attempted to remedy the problem, but two years of low sales only made the problem worse. He was never able to recover.

"I took out a loan and that got us by for a few months, but sales were still low," he said.

She stood in his office, he seated on his desk chair and she on the other side. "You must have gotten another loan." She had gone over the accounting and had seen two loan deposits.

Bernard's face sobered and he didn't answer. He'd been evasive ever since Kendall had learned of the financial troubles.

"Dad, you have to start talking to me." Kendall braced her hands on the edge of her father's desk. "Who else did you borrow money from?"

Bernard got up from his chair and turned to stand at the window, a view of the forest shadowy under an overcast sky.

"I know you did, Dad. Tell me about the Aegis Corporation." She'd searched online and found nothing about them.

"It's a ghost company under the Royal Haven Casino." With a sigh, he walked over to a sitting area with a coffee table and sat.

Kendall went there, as well. Her father had borrowed money from a casino? She sat in the chair next to his.

"I met the owner through a contractor who frequently buys lumber from us," her dad said. "I explained my situation and told him the contractor said he sometimes makes investments."

"He said he did, but it depended on the terms. I thought that was a natural thing to consider when loaning money. He expected to get something out of it."

"What were his terms?" Kendall asked, dreading to hear the answer.

"A percentage of interest and lumber at no cost whenever he requests it."

The interest seemed normal but free lumber whenever he wanted? That sounded extreme. It also seemed like the casino man would keep her father under his thumb for eternity.

"He also said he'd expect timely repayment," her father said.

What kind of casino owner was he? "Let me guess… you were late on a payment."

"The terms were to repay in four installments. I only paid him half of the first and am late on the second."

"I thought the beetle kill lumber helped."

"That's how I came up with half of the first payment. If Emilio Elardi would just agree to give me more time, then I could repay him."

"You asked?"

"Yes. And he said he warned me about his terms. I had to meet them. Period."

"He warned you? What do you mean?" she asked, apprehension building.

"During our second meeting when he had the contract ready, he asked if I was sure I could meet all the terms. At the time I was sure. He went on to say it was important that I did because if I didn't that would interfere with his planning and he didn't like that. He had big plans for the money he'd make on his investment. If I messed that up he wouldn't be happy."

"He said that," Kendall stated without asking. "That he wouldn't be happy." A chill spread through her.

"Yes. I thought it was odd at the time, but the contractor is a good friend of mine. I didn't think he'd send me to anyone questionable."

"He might not know whether Emilio Elardi is questionable or not." A thought came to her. "Has he been in contact with you?"

"Emilio? Not personally. He sends two of his men about once a week, asking for the money I owe."

"That's all? They just ask?"

"In a deceptively friendly way, yes. The last time they came was over two weeks ago, and they told me if I didn't come up with my past-due amounts, Mr. Elardi would be forced to protect his investment."

Whatever that meant. Did Elardi think he could protect his investment by kidnapping Bernard's daughter and demanding payment? The timing was about right. She'd first seen that man a little over two weeks ago. He hadn't actually attempted to kidnap her until later. Mr. Elardi had given Bernard time and then he'd pounced.

A knock on the office door jarred Kendall out of her thoughts. Her father's assistant opened the door.

"Sorry to interrupt," the woman said. "Ms. Hadley, Mr. Decker Colton is here to see you."

"Thank you." Kendall stood. "We'll figure something out, Dad."

He looked up at her with an appreciative look. "I'm more concerned about you."

"I'll be all right." She gave his shoulder a squeeze and left the office.

Decker stood at the assistant's desk, which was in the middle of a square of offices. Hers was in the opposite corner from her father's.

She smiled as she took in Decker's tall, dark and handsome appearance, dressed in a gray suit and purple-and-white tie.

"Hi." She planted a quick kiss on his lips. "What a surprise."

He didn't return her smile. "We need to talk."

Uh-oh. That didn't sound good. She covered her alarm as she stepped back. "All right. Come into my office." Warily she led him there, not having to guess what this was all about.

Decker closed the door behind him and approached her. She braced herself for what was coming.

"I need to ask you something and I need an honest answer."

"Okay. I've always been honest with you."

He blinked, which gave away his doubt. "Is your father in trouble financially?"

She wasn't surprised by his question, but she was reluctant to answer. She had to tell the truth, though.

"Yes," she said, then seeing his profound disappointment, she added, "I didn't know until a few days ago. Remember when you asked what I was talking about with my parents when you were on the phone? That's when I found out."

He watched her with unreadable eyes and no change in his expression. "Your father knew."

"Yes."

"Do you really expect me to believe he didn't tell you?"

"He didn't, Decker. I swear it." She gave him an imploring look. "When he came to me about Russ's proposal, he never mentioned any financial issues."

"You have access to the books, don't you?"

She nodded. "Probably, but that isn't my job. I never looked into the finances."

"Your father must have been too eager to get you to the altar when my father came to him with his idea."

"I've considered that, and yes, I'm not happy about it," she said, unable to argue that her father would have been financially motivated.

"Is that how he talked you into it? Is that why you came to the dinner? To save your family's company?"

"No. I didn't know, Decker." That she had to repeat it said he didn't believe her—at all.

"If you really didn't know until a few days ago, why didn't you tell me?"

She couldn't meet his eyes. Turning, she went to her office window, another view of the forest. Her not telling him right away looked bad.

"I don't know. I suppose I was afraid you'd call off the wedding."

"And if that happened your father's company would be in ruin?" Decker bit out.

She didn't answer right away, hearing the conviction in his tone. "I wasn't sure I wanted you to call it off." She looked back at him. "Not for my father, but for me."

He stared hard at her for a while, as though contemplating whether he believed her or not. "That's what my father wants me to do. Call it off. We had an argument about it this morning."

She turned around to face him fully. "Your father knows?"

"He just found out today."

And then he'd gone to Decker to demand that he call off the wedding. From the sound of it, Decker hadn't agreed to do his father's bidding. He said he and his father argued about calling off the wedding. Had Decker been on the fence? Something in him hadn't immediately wanted to do so. But then, he needed time to think things over. Had he come to a conclusion by now?

"Is that what you're going to do?" she finally asked.

He took a while to answer. "I don't know. The only thing I do know is I'm not going to do what my father tells me to do unless it's what *I* want."

That was new. He must not be afraid of his father taking away his role at The Lodge anymore. But she didn't think he'd go through with the wedding because it no longer made good business sense.

"I didn't know about the money issues at Hadley Forestry when I agreed to marry you," she said.

"It doesn't matter when you found out. The fact is, you did know and didn't tell me."

That was true. "I didn't right away because I was

afraid you wouldn't marry me knowing my family has no money. This is a business deal to you."

He turned to go.

She hadn't expected him to react that way, as though she had insulted him by saying it was only business to him.

"Decker." She followed him to the doorway. "Decker, wait."

"I need time to think," he said over his shoulder. At the elevators, he pressed the down button and turned to look back at her. All she saw was disappointment.

She felt heaviness in her chest, and a lump formed in her throat. She never intended to hurt him. She didn't think that was possible. Did he feel more for her than he let on?

Saddened, she saw the assistant watching and her father standing in the doorway of his own office, looking contrite.

Closing her office door, she went to her desk and put her head in her hands.

Now what?

After being unable to concentrate on work and having to deal with another snobby celebrity, Decker left the office early and now sat at the bar in his rec room, a short glass of whiskey in front of him to take the edge off. The television played but he didn't pay attention. It was more background noise. Kendall not telling him about her father's financial situation bothered him way more than he thought it should.

The money didn't really matter to him, but the notion that she'd intentionally kept him in the dark did.

What he wanted to know was if she had planned to marry him to help her father. If he believed her, then it hadn't started out that way, but he saw no difference whether she had known all along or just a few days ago. Either way, she had deceived him in order to help her father. Would she not have told him until after they were married, to secure the marriage and take her chances on him divorcing her? He didn't trust her answer if he asked.

"Do you still need time?"

He pivoted on the stool to see Kendall standing in the entry of the rec room, still dressed for business in slacks and a blouse. She must have removed the jacket. He didn't like how the impact of her beauty hit him, or her soft, hesitant voice.

"I'm glad you came home," he said, which was true because there was still a madman after her.

She walked into the room and stopped at the bar, taking the stool next to him.

"Something to drink?" he asked.

She eyed his near-empty glass and shook her head. "I don't like to drink when I'm upset."

What did she have to be upset about? The prospect of losing the family business? He had to admit, if he faced the same situation, he'd be a mess. He couldn't imagine losing The Lodge. Sure, it was his dad's vision, but Decker had built it into something grand and successful.

"It's more than not telling you about my father sooner, it's my father too," she said.

He looked at her, seeing earnestness and angst in her eyes.

"This has been going on for a long, long time and he didn't tell anyone. Before I left work, I stopped to see my mother and she told me she didn't know until shortly before I found out. When you were on the phone is when she insisted my father tell me."

Although he resisted believing her, something in him knew she wasn't lying.

"Today he told me who his investors were. One of them is the owner of the Royal Haven Casino, a man named Emilio Elardi. He has a ghost company called Aegis Corporation that loaned my father money. The loan includes some strange terms, like repayment in four installments and free lumber with no limits to how much and for how long."

"A ghost company?" Decker asked. That all sounded strange. Was this casino mogul a gangster? Given that someone had tried to kidnap Kendall, this was beginning to make more sense.

Kendall curled her hands on the bar surface, looking down at them in distress. "My father said Emilio sends two of his men to see him on a regular basis, demanding payment. They warned him that Mr. Elardi would protect his investment if he had to."

"Hence the man sent to kidnap you." Anger welled up toward a man who would dare harm someone close to him. No legitimate bank would conduct business that way, with dangerous threats.

She looked up at him. "Yes."

"Why didn't Bernard go to a traditional bank?" Decker asked.

"He did. They won't loan him anymore."

Because he was that deep in debt. Decker ran his fingers through his hair. His father would really love to hear that.

"I just found out about the casino this morning," she said.

He knew she'd told him that with the hope he believed her, to show him that she was being honest.

"I came here to tell you that," she said. "And also to tell you I'm calling off the wedding."

"Kendall…" What could he say? He wasn't sure he even wanted to go through with marriage now.

"I don't want to marry you with you wondering if I'm doing it for money," she murmured sincerely.

"We're not calling off anything." Not yet anyway. He still needed more time to think. He was confused over how much her deception had affected him. He couldn't recall if he had ever had such an emotional reaction to any other woman. He didn't think so, which bothered him, and he couldn't explain to himself why…

"Then have a prenuptial agreement drawn up by your lawyers. I'll sign it," Kendall said.

She'd do that? His father might go along with something like that, except his terms would be a lot harsher than anything Decker would draw up. Decker would not leave her penniless if they ended up divorced. He'd make sure she would be all right financially. As far as her father and Hadley Forestry went, he could control that while they were married.

"I think it's best if I move back into my own house for now," she said.

"No." Decker swiveled to face her and clasped her hands in his. He leaned closer. "No, Kendall. I want you here. I have good security. You'll be safe."

"But I think you need time to—"

"No. You're staying."

She angled her head and he read her dislike of his order.

"Please," he added. "Stay. In my bed if you want, or in another room. Your choice. I just want you here so I know you're safe. The casino owner sounds dangerous, more dangerous than we thought. He hired a professional. Stay, Kendall. Will you?"

"How can I refuse when you ask like that?" She smiled a little, but sadness remained in her eyes.

"My strong, stubborn woman." He moved in to kiss her.

She kissed him back and the flames quickly spread. He withdrew to stave the sexual hunger. Now was not the time for that.

Chapter 10

Sheriff Colton and Deputy Sheriff Bloom showed up the following morning. Kendall's father had phoned in what he knew about Emilio Elardi.

"Decker," Trey greeted. "Kendall."

Kendall shook his hand and then Daria's.

"We're seeing entirely too much of you two lately," Kendall said.

"Yes." Daria turned to Decker. "And still nothing new to report on the Rouge murder."

"No need for a status call this week, then," Decker replied.

"Your father filled me in on Emilio Elardi," Trey said to Kendall, all business. He had a serious expression and she wondered if he smiled very often. Decker was the same way, except with her. She noticed with other people his body language never revealed much, especially with his father.

"I did a preliminary background check and received some alarming information," Trey went on.

Kendall felt her breath seize for a second. *Alarming?* She did not want to be right about her father's dealings with the casino owner. Sensing Decker glance at her, she met his gaze and saw his brow gradually becoming stormy. Did protectiveness of her put that look there?

"Elardi has been in trouble with the law before," Daria said.

"And some other incidents have been linked to him as well," Trey added.

Kendall controlled a surge of frustration. How could her father have missed the type of character Emilio was? Bernard was not a stupid man. He was an entrepreneur. An Ivy League grad. Leader all the way. She didn't understand how this could have happened. It was as though he'd been hoodwinked into this deal.

"A woman arrested for drug dealing claimed she worked for him," Trey said.

"And an informant relating to that arrest claimed Elardi was linked to a drug cartel in Mexico," Daria added.

"What does that have to do with Kendall's attack?" Decker asked, more like demanded.

Trey remained calm and unreflective. "Maybe nothing, but he's also got a record of domestic abuse. His wife called for help and said to the dispatcher that he hit her after an argument."

"They were fighting about money," Daria went on

to say. "Apparently she wanted more control over how and when she spent money and he refused."

Either Elardi was a control freak or he hadn't wanted his wife to know something about his finances. Had she caught on to his illicit deals? What if her attempt to have more control over spending was her way of trying to get him to talk?

"What is particularly noteworthy is the wife mysteriously disappeared shortly thereafter," Trey said. "She was last seen at her hairdresser's shop. Emilio had an airtight alibi."

That was significant. Elardi must have had something to do with her disappearance.

"Would Elardi have been charged with domestic abuse?" Decker asked.

"He was arrested and got out on bond," Trey said. "His wife never had a chance to press charges."

Kendall looked at Decker as they both processed that powerful piece of information. They must be dealing with a very dangerous man.

"That's not all," Daria said. "There is another missing person case involving a ransom demand."

Kendall gasped, truly afraid now. Elardi had done it before? And the victim was never returned. *Missing person...*

"The victim's family worked with the FBI to arrange the ransom drop," Daria told them. "They were instructed to leave the money at a specified location and then go to another location where the kidnappers claimed the victim would be left. But she never was dropped off there and her body has not been found."

Kendall felt sick to her stomach.

"They had agents at both locations," Trey added. "The agent at the drop saw a man dressed in black and wearing mask take the bag and run. He got on a motorcycle about a block away and escaped."

"That was a true ransom case," Decker said. "It wasn't a case were the victim's family owned money. Is that right?"

Trey shook his head. "No. They owed a hundred thousand. The ransom was for one-fifty."

"What's interesting about that case," Daria said, "is the victim's family was referred to Elardi by someone they knew."

"Who?" Decker asked.

"He's a general contractor."

"That's how my father got in touch with Elardi," Kendall said.

"We're going to talk to him this afternoon," Trey said. "It's still not clear if he's involved. He might be referring without knowledge of the kind of businessman Elardi is."

That's what she and her father had discussed, but what if the contractor was paid by Elardi to generate *business*?

"Why wasn't Elardi arrested?" Kendall asked.

"There's no proof. The agreement between parties is legitimate. There is no proof linking Elardi to the kidnapping or the ransom."

That figured. Until they had confirmation, Kendall could only assume Elardi had similar plans for her in order to force her father to pay.

* * *

The next day, Decker went to work, burdened by thoughts of Kendall. Decker didn't think her living by herself was smart right now and was glad he'd invited her to continue to stay with him. Despite their conflict at the moment—or his current inability to trust her—he would see that she was safe. She agreed and he couldn't tell if she had done so out of interest in him or concern for her life. He wasn't ready to trust her, didn't know if he ever would, but he also wasn't ready to let her go.

Around lunchtime, a knock on the office door preceded Russ entering. At least he had knocked.

Decker searched for signs of his dad's mood and sensed neutrality. For now.

"Any progress on increasing reservations?" Russ asked.

"I've got a meeting with Remy later this week. He may have some ideas."

"He's a good public relations director for The Chateau."

His father stood there on the other side of Decker's desk, seeming to be thinking something over.

"About our last meeting," Russ said. "I was just upset over hearing the news about the Hadleys. I was so excited about you and Kendall seeming like such a good pair that it got to me."

Decker couldn't form a response. His dad was apologizing? Was he worried Decker would walk away from the company? Then again, it didn't really sound like a full apology.

"It's all right. I wasn't happy, either."

"On that subject. Have you given some thought to postponing?"

He at least wanted Decker to postpone the wedding. "I haven't decided yet, Dad. Kendall and I do get along well—or we did before all this." Decker paused as his disappointment returned along with the uncertainty as to whether he could trust her or not.

"Yes, it's a lot to take in. But, son, I really think you'd be better off not marrying her."

With his father saying that in a calmer voice, Decker took it to heart. "I'm considering all options."

"Did she know about the Hadley Forestry problems when I brought up the idea of the two of you marrying?"

Decker had to be honest. "She claims not to."

"You don't believe her, do you? This was going to be an arranged marriage. She obviously cares more for her family than you."

Decker took a deep, slow breath, disturbed because his father did have a valid point. Kendall would naturally care more about the welfare of her family than him. She hadn't been with him much. She couldn't possibly have had enough time with him to grow to care for him on that level.

"I know she seemed wonderful at first," his dad continued, "but think of the future of The Colton Empire. Think of our reputation."

Reputation. What he'd learned about Kendall's father didn't bode well for Hadley Forestry's reputation. If it got out—and it would—that Bernard had done business with a crooked casino owner, the consequences would be dire. Decker could be brought down with them, or at least suffer a revenue impact as a result.

"I discovered Bernard went into business with a casino. What's the story with that?" his dad asked.

How had he found that out? Decker didn't ask. He also did not feel like getting into that with his father. "You'll have to ask him."

Russ sat on the edge of the desk. "Will you at least cool things off with Kendall?"

"I already have." He hadn't exactly told her that but he had distanced himself.

"But she's still living with you, mooching off you."

Mooching? Kendall made her own income. He wouldn't say she had taken advantage of him, yet. When Hadley Forestry went down, then she'd be set up under the Colton umbrella.

"She has a stalker."

Russ nodded. "I heard about that. She's a big girl. She can take care of herself. Get rid of her before she really turns your life upside down. We don't need that kind of trash in the family right now. We're still recovering from that Rouge murder."

Decker didn't respond. He didn't appreciate his father's semantics, but he wasn't in the mood for another argument.

"Think of the business, son."

"I am, Dad. I won't let anything damage The Lodge any more than what's already been done. You have my word on that."

"Good. I know you were interested in investing in Hadley Forestry but thank goodness we found out about their scandal. We have too many high-class connections. A woman like Kendall might drive a wedge into those important relationships."

A woman like Kendall? His father talked about her as though she grew up in a depraved family. "Like I said, I've cooled it off with her. Be happy with that, Dad." Decker needed his father to back off. "When her stalker is caught, I'll address the situation at that time."

Seeing a satisfied look come over Russ, Decker was sure he had said the magic words.

"You see what I mean, don't you?" Russ asked. "Kendall may have grown up privileged, but that life is over for her. She no longer fits into the Colton way of life."

Decker leaned back, amazed how his father could talk in such a calm tone and say such nasty things about people. When everything *fit* and went according to his script, he was a decent man to be with. His Colton Empire had gone to his head somewhere along the way. Decker liked the rich lifestyle they lived, but he would never look at others less fortunate and pass judgment the way his father did.

Kendall had decided she was certain she wanted to pursue marriage with Decker. She felt enough for him to make it worthwhile and she wouldn't lose him because of a misunderstanding. She planned to have a long talk with him, and if he still didn't believe her then she'd keep working on him until he did. Her instincts told her this was a good match. She could trust him not to betray her, even if he entered into their marriage for business reasons.

She reached his office, where his assistant was absent from her desk.

Stepping up to Decker's office door, she stopped when she heard Russ Colton talking about investing in Hadley Forestry. The office door was open and she stood out of sight. She heard Russ say, "She obviously cares more for her family than you."

She listened more, feeling a sting prick her heart.

"Think of our reputation."

Decker didn't say anything to that, which further stung Kendall.

"Will you at least cool things off with Kendall?" she heard Russ ask.

"I already have."

He had? He hadn't told her that. Kendall had to control her breathing. She heard the conversation go on, picking up on snippets that pricked her heart some more.

"…mooching off you."

"She's a big girl…"

"Get rid of her before she really turns your life upside down."

Decker again said nothing. Kendall could not believe it. It was as though he silently agreed with his father.

"Think if the business, son."

"I am, Dad. I won't let anything damage The Lodge any more than what's already been done. You have my word on that."

"A woman like Kendall might drive a wedge into those important relationships."

"Like I said, I've cooled it off with her. Be happy with that, Dad."

Kendall covered her mouth to silence a shocked exhale.

"She no longer fits into the Colton way of life."

Kendall waited for Decker to say something in her defense, but he didn't. How could he possibly think she'd drag him down, ruin his reputation? He really must only look at her like an asset, except now she was no longer an asset.

"Did you see the numbers in the weekly report?" Decker asked, drastically changing the subject.

He had completely dismissed Kendall and set his mind on work. That's how easy it was for him to close himself off to women. He acted like he cared but it was all a show. Now that she was no longer wealthy, she didn't matter.

Kendall heard Russ pat Decker once. "I was worried about you, but now I'm certain you're the man I need in charge here."

"You know how much this company means to me. You should never doubt that," Decker said.

Kendall felt sick to her stomach, much more than when she'd learned of the other ransom case. She didn't need to hear more. She also didn't want Decker to know what she'd heard. He obviously felt nothing for her. All he cared about was his company. And apparently, still pleasing his father.

Leaving the office door, she almost bumped into Decker's assistant.

"Hi, Kendall. Did you need to see Decker?"

"No." She walked quickly toward the elevator.

How could she have been so wrong about him? He had put on quite a show, wooing her, making her believe he was honest and sincere when all he had wanted to do was secure the deal, merge the wealthy Hadleys with the wealthy Coltons. A perfect pairing.

All the way down to the lobby she fought the sting of tears. She all but ran to her vehicle. Alone inside, she couldn't fight her emotion any longer. She started crying, wiping tears as she raced to the highway, not understanding the intensity of her reaction.

She didn't love him so why should it hurt so much to hear him talking to his father about her like that? Or *not* talking? It was the things he hadn't said that hurt the most. When he had spoken his tone had been even and a little low, as though disappointment had taken some steam out of him. Kendall, his ideal wifey, turned out to be a farce. A bad deal after all. Her father treated her the same way, different because he was her father but she had never liked feeling like an asset more than a daughter.

Also, Decker's shunning hurt because it felt very similar to when she had caught the man she had lived with in bed with another woman. She hated thinking she'd never find love, hated even more how sad that made her, and how inadequate. The latter was the worst. She wasn't a weak person, but Decker had just made her feel that way.

She arrived at Decker's and hurried to pack her things.

Decker pulled up to Kendall's house about an hour after his dad had left his office. They had talked numbers for a few minutes and then his dad had left. His assistant had come into his office to get his signature on some documents and asked him if he'd seen Kendall.

"Kendall was here?"

"Yes, I ran into her when she was on her way to the elevators. She seemed to be in a hurry."

He had gone on hyperalert then.

"She said she didn't need to see you, which I thought was strange," his assistant had said.

So did he. Or not. She must have decided not to see him after she'd heard him talking with his dad. Russ Colton had not said anything nice about her.

Decker had first checked at home but Kendall had already taken her things and left. Now he stood outside her front door, ringing the doorbell for the second time.

She didn't answer. Her Land Rover was in the garage—he'd checked. She was inside, just ignoring him.

"Kendall?" he said loud enough for her to hear on the other side of the door. "I know you're in there."

She didn't answer. He left the door and walked to the side, then around back. She had no fence, which made him worry even more about her safety. Reaching her patio and two French doors, he could see inside. A six-seat round table filled a casual dining area. To the left, two kitchen islands with gray countertops were in the center of three walls of white cabinets with gray knobs and stainless steel appliances. These doors and a large arched window over the sink area brightened the room. He could see part of the living room from here. Kendall stood in the middle, looking right at him.

He lifted a hand in greeting.

She folded her arms and stuck out a foot.

"Let me in, Kendall," he said loudly.

She didn't move.

"I'm not leaving until you do," he insisted.

Dropping her hands in exasperation, she walked to the back door and let him in.

He stepped in and stood just inside the kitchen. She had stepped back and now had one hand on the first kitchen island top.

"You heard me talking with my father today," he said.

She pursed her lips and her brow raised as though saying a silent, "Yes and I'm not happy."

"He can be a little difficult to bear at times," he said.

"You didn't disagree with him," she retorted and he heard the edginess in her tone.

"I didn't want to argue with him."

"Right because pleasing him is more important to you than me." She lifted both hands, palms facing Decker. "You know what? Forget it. It doesn't matter. We're finished. I don't want to see you ever again."

Ever? "Kendall. I don't agree with what my dad said."

"You don't? Not even the part where he said I might drive a wedge into important relationships? Those wealthy and famous customers of yours?"

"No, I especially don't agree with that," he said.

"Really? What if it gets out that my father did business with a criminal?" she asked. "That won't be good publicity for your business."

He couldn't deny that and he didn't now.

"I'm not *fit* to be part of the Colton family," she said.

"Now that I don't agree with. You are fit, Kendall. You aren't responsible for what your father did."

"Thanks, that makes everything so much better," she said sarcastically.

"I know it sounded bad," he admitted. "My father can be rather pompous at times. He'll get over it."

"He won't have to, Decker. As you said, you've cooled things off with me. The only reason you're here is out of guilt. You don't want my stalker to hurt me."

"That is not the only reason I'm here. I want you to come back to my house."

She scoffed. "Oh, that is not going to happen. I officially absolve you of any responsibility for my well-being. You can go back to jumping whenever your father tells you to."

"I'm not jumping when he tells me to."

"Why did you say you cooled things off with me?"

"Because I have." He ran his fingers through his hair with a sigh. How could he explain?

"It would have been nice if you could have told me that," she said.

"I just need a little time."

"For what? The wedding is off, Decker. I'm not marrying you."

He stared at her, realizing she meant it. She would not marry him. That told him a lot about her character—namely that he might have been a fool to doubt her.

"Let's take a few days to calm down. I haven't written us off yet and neither should you. Screw what my dad says. Screw what he thinks. He thinks too much of the bottom line. And despite what you imagine, I am not doing anything for him anymore. I follow my own creed. That includes any decisions I make regarding you."

"Well, I follow my own creed, too, and I will not marry you. Please leave now."

Had he really lost her? He wasn't ready to. "Kendall…"

"Please, Decker. I know you were only marrying me for your business and that is no longer a good deal. Why else would you marry me?"

"I like you. We get along so well. You're perfect for me. And we were going to have a family."

She stared at him this time, her face no longer so stiff with anger and upset. She seemed more resolved than ever.

"After hearing what I heard, that is no longer enough for me," she said.

Now she wanted more. She wanted the real thing. Love. How could he make her love him in the short time they had until the end of the month? He didn't have to love her. He loved being with her.

"And I won't be anyone's asset anymore."

"You were never an asset to me," Decker rasped, but inside he felt the inaccuracy of that declaration. She would have been an asset to him. He had treated her that way more than once, and it shamed him to realize it now. He'd put his business first—all because he didn't believe he'd ever find true love.

"I never meant to treat you that way," he amended. "I know my business is important to me, but you've come to mean much more to me than a transaction, that much I can say honestly."

He saw her blink slowly, as though he'd finally reached through her layers of hurt.

"It was never only about joining two good families," he added. "Family was always part of the equation. That and a solid companionship, which I know we will have."

"I'm not going to live with you, Decker," she said. "And right now I still am certain I'm not marrying you. Not at the end of the month, anyway."

That was something. At least she'd eased off adamantly refusing to marry him—ever.

Chapter 11

Decker left Kendall alone over the next two days. Today, she arrived at her office to six full bouquets of red roses and baby's breath. There was a card in one.

Dinner? it read.

"He seems pretty determined."

Kendall saw her mother enter as she turned from the vase on her desk. She smiled, dropping the card to go to her for a brief hug.

"What brings you by?" Kendall asked.

"I wanted to talk to you about your father." Marion sat on the love seat in Kendall's office. Kendall joined her there.

"Are you all right?" her mother asked.

"Yes."

"You haven't been seeing Decker."

"No."

Her mother glanced around the office. "What's all this?"

"He asked me to dinner."

"Are you going to go?"

"I don't know." As she thought it over, she knew she was too interested to refuse. "Probably." She took out her cell phone and texted Decker, Yes.

He immediately responded with, I'll pick you up at five. It will take us a little while to get to the restaurant.

Where was he taking her?

"Have you heard the talk around town?" her mother asked.

"No. Do I want to know?"

"It appears Russ Colton is spreading rumors that Decker broke off the engagement and is going to marry someone else."

"Who?" The news gave her heart a jolt, a stinging one. The Decker she had gotten to know wouldn't do that, but she had only been seeing him a short while. And given her bad experience with Gabe.

"A celebrity. I don't know which one. It's also all over town that your father is crooked, partnering with a gangster." She looked upset about that.

Kendall figured the latter was her father's own doing. She pitied him but not much more.

As for Decker being with a celebrity, she supposed she could believe that. He enjoyed the glamorous success of The Lodge.

"He didn't mean for any of this to happen," her mother said. "He jumped into that deal with Emilio too quickly. He loves this company so much. It's his baby. He'd have done anything to save it, probably still will."

"Yes, he's made that abundantly clear. Marrying me off to Decker was my first clue."

"Keeping secret what he found out about Emilio is another. But it is what it is, Kendall. We as a family have to make it right again."

Her mother made good sense. If they could clear up the snafu with Emilio and find a way out of debt, they could rebuild the company and its reputation.

A commotion outside the office brought her attention away from her mother. Her assistant was telling a courier that Kendall wasn't expecting any packages.

"I just do the deliveries, ma'am." The delivery man left.

Kendall stood, growing suspicious. "Mary, step back from that package. Wait over here by my office." She could not be too cautious right now.

Mary went to stand next to Kendall's mother.

Kendall went to inspect the package. She didn't recognize the return address. She picked it up and shook it. Something rattled inside, but only slightly. It didn't weigh much, but wasn't light, maybe five pounds.

"Let's call security." She turned and walked back toward her office. Mary and her mother waited there, standing close and looking afraid.

Before Kendall reached them, an explosion erupted.

Kendall felt the pressure of it at her back and stumbled, falling forward and rolling. She heard her mother scream and Mary shout out. Mary reached her first, kneeling to drag her into the office and to presumed safety.

"Are you all right?" her mother asked, frantic and falling to her knees beside her.

Kendall made note of her body, not feeling anything detrimental. "I think so."

Her assistant called 911 while her mother touched her all over and inspected her. Kendall was all right. The explosion had been loud and strong but it hadn't destroyed the room, not completely. If she'd have had her hands on the box, she'd have been injured but not killed. The bomber intended for her to be all right.

In the next five minutes, emergency personnel arrived, swarming around her and checking her to be sure she wasn't hurt. Kendall still felt dazed and incredulous that her stalker would courier her a bomb.

City police arrived and an officer approached Kendall, her mother and her assistant, who had gone into Kendall's office. Kendall acknowledged law enforcement's need to talk to her, seeing other officers were with her mother and her assistant. She explained the background of her stalker and that the sheriff's office was handling it due to the assailant's stolen car being found outside the city limits.

"We'll work collaboratively with the sheriff's office," the policeman said.

Kendall saw Decker appear in the doorway of her office. He rushed to her.

"Are you all right?" He crouched before her, taking her hands and surveying her.

"I'm all right. How did you get here so quickly?"

Kendall felt her mother observe them closely and with interest.

"Trey called. He heard the radio communications."

Tight-knit family. She was warmed that he'd dropped everything and come to her side. She didn't think it was for show. No, it couldn't be. Her family was broke. He'd come for her.

"Are you hurt?" He checked her all over again. "Anywhere?"

"No. I'm okay, just a little shaken."

"It was another warning," her mother said.

"Would anyone like some coffee?" Kendall's assistant asked.

"I'd love one," Marion said.

"Thank you," Kendall said.

The assistant left and Kendall saw that Trey had arrived, standing beside the officer who'd questioned her, talking.

"This is getting so scary," Kendall's mother said. "Why is Emilio going after you? Why not Bernard?" Marion's blue eyes glimmered with worry.

"To make him suffer," Decker retorted and then turned to Kendall. "It's not safe for you anywhere."

She could not disagree. Elardi had sent his henchman to her workplace. What would he do next?

Bernard arrived, having been out for a meeting. Breathless and with wide, frantic eyes, he came to Kendall.

"Oh, thank goodness. You're all right." He reached her and bent to kiss her forehead. Then he straightened. "Emilio called me. He said next time she won't get away. He said I wouldn't be visiting my daughter in a hospital."

So Elardi had planned on sending Kendall to the hospital? Good thing he failed again. He might feel confident that he could succeed in kidnapping her, but so far his attempts had failed.

Decker stood up. "I think she should stay with me."

"I think so too," Bernard said.

Kendall sent him a warning look. Was he still angling for her to land a marriage with a wealthy Colton? She saw her mother with a similar expression. Kendall observed Decker and couldn't tell what he thought. He watched her, waiting for a reaction, no doubt.

She wouldn't jump in and say, "Sure." He'd only have her for as long as she was in danger. They'd already been over that. He had to know she hadn't changed her mind. She could stay with her parents but then she might put them in danger, as well.

Outside the office, bomb experts had finished examining the explosive device and Trey entered Kendall's office.

"How are we doing?" he asked as he came to a stop beside Decker.

"Okay for now."

"Bomb squad confirmed it was an M-80, a little more boom than a firecracker but enough to cause injury to hands and face," Trey said. "Meant to scare you not kill you. You were lucky."

Lucky in that she had begun to walk away from the box before it exploded. She wouldn't say she was completely lucky because Elardi was still after her.

"That's what we thought too," Kendall said.

"I don't think she should be alone," Decker pressed.

"I'd have to agree," Trey said.

"I do, too, honey," her mother added. "Why don't you accept Decker's offer to stay with him? He's done a good job protecting you up to this point."

What would she do? She wasn't safe at work. She wasn't safe at home, not alone anyway. Decker was right. She wasn't safe anywhere. He had a fence around his property and cameras, much more robust than her security system.

"I'll stay in a room at the Lodge," she finally said.

"Fair enough," Decker said. "The Lodge has twenty-four-seven security. As long as you promise me you won't go anywhere without telling me."

She could agree to that. "All right."

Decker couldn't stop thinking about Kendall. It was more than the danger she was in; he missed being with her. It had only been two days since the bomb incident. He had left her alone for the most part. Today he'd reached his limit. He didn't understand why he had to see her, but he just did. He sent her flowers again to try to make up for the fact that they had missed their dinner date, and he'd already instructed the staff to see to her every need. She had room service at her beck and call.

He spotted Liam Kastor enter the administration area of his office space. His assistant came into his office.

"Send him in," Decker said before she had a chance to announce Liam's arrival.

Tall with a youthful face at thirty-three, he had blond

hair and light green eyes and an intelligent look about him. Since he was a detective for the Roaring Springs Police Department, Decker was more than a little curious as to why he was here.

Decker stood and came around his desk to meet him in the middle. He shook the man's hand.

"Thanks for seeing me without an appointment," Liam said.

"It's the least I can do for my soon-to-be brother-in-law. How are you and Sloane doing, anyway?"

"Great. We set a wedding date. I should probably let her tell you but we'd like you to come. It will be a small ceremony."

"I wouldn't miss it."

"I don't think she's gotten past you getting engaged to a woman Russ picked," Liam said. "How is that going?"

"We ran into a small hiccup, but I am sure we'll get back on track."

"Yeah, everybody's heard about the Hadleys going in debt to that casino owner. Is he really a criminal?"

"It looks that way. Both the police and Trey and his team are looking into it."

"Sloane said your dad won't let you marry Kendall now."

"He doesn't have a say."

Liam drew back a little, seeming surprised. "Aren't you concerned what he'll do?"

"I am, but I've made a decision about that and I'm sticking to it."

Liam whistled. "Wow, that's not the Decker Colton that Sloane told me about."

"You mean the one that does everything Russ says? Yeah, not anymore, thanks to Kendall. She's opened my eyes to a lot of things."

Liam nodded with a grin. "I know how that goes. Love has a way of sneaking up on a man."

Decker felt Liam's last statement sting. Love? Sneaking up? That wasn't happening to him. He had a very organized approach to his relationship with Kendall. She would make him a great wife. Period. The best he'd ever find, probably. He couldn't be more satisfied with his choice, but love? No. He still wasn't convinced.

"What brought you by today, Liam?" Decker asked.

Liam chuckled. "I get it, bro. Don't want to talk about it." He reached into his jacket pocket and took out some photographs. "I'm investigating a missing person case."

Decker took the first photo and thought he was looking at a picture of Bianca Rouge.

"That's April Thomas," Liam said. "She came to Roaring Springs to try to find a job and disappeared instead. Her mother came here looking for her. Since she has a striking resemblance to Bianca, I wanted to see if you or anyone else here at The Lodge recognize her."

"Striking resemblance for sure. People will probably mistake her for Bianca."

"I'm afraid of that, but I'm hoping someone will notice a difference."

Liam showed him another photo. In this one, Decker could see the difference between the two women.

April's hair was a little different than Bianca's and so were the features of her face.

"I haven't seen anyone who looks like Bianca," Decker said. "But I can take you around and you can show that to others." He led Liam out of the office and down a hall.

He found Molly Gilford, Decker's director of guest relations. A marriage between her aunt Mara and Russ had joined the two families together. She didn't have any hard feelings about being employed by a Colton and Decker had tremendous respect for her work ethic and her efficiency. Guests all liked her, which was a definite plus. If anyone had had a chance to spot April, Molly would have.

"Hi, Decker," she greeted in her friendly way. Curvy and pretty with a blond bob and blue eyes, she smiled in his direction then turned to Liam.

Decker explained why he was here and Liam showed her the pictures.

"No, I'm sorry, I don't recognize her. But you say she was job hunting here in Roaring Springs?"

"Yes," Liam said.

"Let me take you to Human Resources then."

"I'll go with you." Decker walked with them down a wide hall. Reaching HR, Molly introduced Liam to the director of personnel, Curtis Shruggs. A thin but fit man of average build with dark peppered gray hair, his bright blue eyes looked up from behind his desk. Seeing Decker, he stood and came around to greet them.

"Decker."

"Hello, Curtis." Decker didn't stop by to see Curtis

very often. "This is Detective Kastor. He's investigating a missing person case."

Liam showed him the photos while Molly took up a conversation with Curtis's fifty-year-old assistant, Shelly Bates.

"Have you ever seen this woman?" Liam asked.

"No, I haven't," Curtis answered.

Liam took the photo over to Shelly and asked her the same question. She and Molly stopped talking as Liam showed her the photos.

Shelly inspected the photo for several seconds. "Yes, I think I remember her." She looked up from the pictures. "Yup, that's her. At least, I think it is. What about her?"

"She went missing," Liam said.

"Oh." Shelly's face sobered. "That's terrible."

"Was she a guest here?" Molly asked, using the assistant's computer to look something up.

"No. She came to The Lodge a little more than a year ago. I gave her an application but she never brought it back."

"That's why her name isn't in our system," Molly said.

"Are you sure this woman is April?" Liam asked.

She hadn't seemed certain.

"She does look like the woman I gave the application to, but it's been such a long time."

"Thank you," Liam said. "You've been a big help."

Decker glanced back to see Curtis looking on. He didn't say anything and seemed anxious. To get back to work?

"Why don't I take you around to the other departments?" Molly said. "Maybe someone else saw her."

"Good idea."

"I'll leave you in Molly's capable hands," Decker said. "I've got to get back to work."

As he headed toward his office, he wondered if another woman had fallen victim to a killer. Was someone targeting women who looked like Bianca Rouge?

Kendall had not imagined she'd like staying at The Lodge as much as she did. Decker had put her in the same room they'd shared before, his suite. Room service delivered meals quickly and the food was outstanding. She had taken the gondola to The Chateau and spent a good portion of her second day there. She had told Decker where she was going, as requested, and he'd sent a security guard with her.

Now she stepped into the opulent lobby and spotted him standing near the elevators, waiting for her. In a light blue-gray suit with a white shirt and no tie, he looked devastatingly handsome.

She had gone on the casual side as well in white pants with a white silky blouse and a black-and-white scarf. For shoes she's opted for high-heels.

Decker offered his arm and she slipped hers into the opening. When he smiled down at her as he escorted her to the restaurant, her heartbeat quickened in response. She was really looking forward to this dinner with him and hoped the time together would help ease some of the tension between them.

Crystal chandeliers and authentic paintings decorated the open room of linen-topped tables. Waitresses and waiters walked in black-and-white uniforms and the rich and famous talked in moderate tones.

Decker took her to a private table in a corner and near a window with a view of ski slopes during the day. Now dark outside, she could only see the exterior lights shining down on a courtyard.

"Thanks for joining me for dinner," Decker said.

"I don't have a lot to do now that I'm on leave from my job," she said, not meaning to sound like she'd accepted because she was bored. "I mean…"

"It's okay. How was your day at The Chateau?"

She smiled with the memory. "I think I could turn into a pampered woman."

"You could if you marry me."

She grew uncomfortable. Clearly he still thought about getting married. She just didn't understand why. Or if he really meant it.

"Let's forget about the arranged marriage," Decker said. "Let's just start over."

"You want that?" Kendall had a hard time believing that. Why had he had a change of heart?

"Yes."

"But I thought you didn't believe you'd ever fall in love."

"I still don't," he admitted gruffly. "All I know is I miss being with you all the time. I don't want to lose that. And remember, I still want a family. I already told you marriage means more to me than a good business move."

"Being with me will not be a good business move,"

she reminded him. Would she be lining herself up for another relationship that ended badly? She had thought her last serious boyfriend had loved her. If Decker ever told her he loved her, she couldn't be sure she'd believe him.

"I can make it into one," Decker said. "Or I'll enjoy the challenge of trying."

"Your father will never support that."

"Maybe not."

"He won't support you marrying me, either."

A muscle ticked in his jaw. "That's not up to him. I may have agreed to his idea but it was always my decision to marry you, and it still is."

"He could take your position away."

"He won't. I might walk away, though. If he keeps trying to dictate my life, I will."

Kendall heard his certainty, his confidence and saw it on his handsome face, in his dark, warm eyes. She loved that about him.

When she'd first agreed to the arranged marriage, she had thought she'd be safe. She had thought her heart would be safe. But she no longer felt that way. Now she feared she could and would fall in love with Decker, which would lead to the same disaster as she'd suffered in the past.

"I don't know, Decker."

"We still have time."

She smiled. "Not much." The end of the month was fast approaching.

"Liam Kastor stopped by today," Decker said.

"Ah." She frowned. "Why did he stop by?"

"To ask about a missing person case. The woman looks a lot like the call girl who was killed, the one who stayed at The Lodge."

"Oh. Do you think the two cases are related?"

"That's what's been bothering me ever since Liam showed me the victim's pictures."

Kendall was flattered that he felt comfortable enough to talk to her about this. It seemed he needed to share it with someone and he trusted her enough to do so with her.

"She was going to apply for a job at The Lodge," Decker said. "But she never got the chance. She disappeared."

"If they're related there could be a serial killer in Roaring Springs," Kendall said.

"Yeah. That's what troubles me. It's terrible that Bianca was murdered and this new woman has gone missing, but another negative publicity stunt will hurt business even more."

Decker cared what happened to the missing girl, but Bianca had stayed at his lodge and now this missing woman had been there, as well. She'd gone missing after picking up an application for a job.

"Has anyone else seen her? Did the detective ask several people?"

"Yes, he asked several. None that he spoke to recognized her other than Shelly Bates, one of our HR employees."

Their conversation moved on to other topics and Kendall found it no coincidence that they could talk so easily together. She could almost finish his thoughts and he hers.

After dinner, Decker walked with her to the elevators.

"Do you want to go up with me?" she asked, not wanting the night to end. She'd truly felt a connection to him and she could tell he felt the same—whether he intended to or not. He may not believe in mad, passionate love, but she did and she wanted to see where this led.

"Are you sure?" he asked quietly.

"Yes." They'd already slept together. Why should she deprive herself of something that made her feel so good?

Heart be damned.

He stepped into the elevator after her and she didn't look away from his heating eyes. He stood close and held her gaze all the way up to her floor.

In the hall, he walked beside her, not touching her— yet. Kendall loved what a gentleman he was.

She opened her suite door and went inside with him. He stepped in behind her. The door closed and she vowed to keep the rest of the world and all her worries and fears on the other side.

Decker removed his jacket, walking to the sitting area and draping it over the arm of a sofa. Kendall kicked off her shoes and went to change into something more comfortable. Taking off her pants and blouse, she reached for a long-sleeved nightgown and then stopped when she saw a much less modest one. This one dipped low in the front and was sleeveless and a little sheer.

She put that one on. Maybe it was the dinner with

Decker; maybe it was just being with him and sensing his softening. But she wanted to look sexy for him.

When she emerged from the room, she saw that Decker had turned on the gas fireplace. He had unbuttoned his shirt about a third of the way and was barefooted, standing in front of a sofa.

Seeing her, he stared with hot eyes. Satisfied that she had achieved her desired result, she walked toward him. She was glad he had turned on the fireplace.

Sitting on the sofa, he patted the space beside him and she did as he invited. He put his feet up on the coffee table and his arm around her. She snuggled closer, unable to deny how right this felt. Nothing else mattered.

She tipped her head back to find him looking at her. Their eyes met and then he kissed her softly. His warm, sweet breath touched her skin as he caressed her with his lips. He didn't take the kiss deeper, only lingered in the simmering passion. She slipped her hand inside his shirt and felt his hard chest.

When he withdrew, he slid his arm beneath her and with his other arm already at her back, lifted her. Kendall enjoyed just looking at his face as he carried her to the bedroom.

Letting her feet down, he stepped back and undressed while she watched.

"Aren't you going to get undressed?" he asked.

She shook her head. "No. I want you to do it."

His passion tightened his jaw and put more fire in his eyes as he looked down her body. "Are you wearing anything under that?"

"You're going to have to come here and find out."

Naked, he did just that. He came to stand before her and lifted the nightgown over her head to find her nude underneath.

Kendall loved the ravaging hunger in his eyes as they looked their fill and then met hers. He took her hair in his hand and tipped her head back and kissed her firmer than before. Stepping forward, he backed her to the bed and followed her down. She lost herself in the gripping love they made from there, with him restraining himself long enough to take things slow until neither of them could hold off any longer.

Then he thrust into her several times until both of them were breathless and deliciously sated.

Kendall's last thought before curling up against him was how in the world she would ever get over such a man if she ever had to. She hoped she never would, but one thing she knew is there were no certainties in life.

Chapter 12

Decker awoke to loud knocking. He felt Kendall stir beside him, lying on her side with one leg over his and her hand on his chest. He felt her nakedness all the way down his length and began to respond. Someone pounded on the room door again.

He eased away from her as she began to open her eyes. Checking the time, he wondered who had the gall to knock on the door at this early hour—just after six in the morning. He and Kendall hadn't fallen asleep until late last night, and what a night it had been. She had let down her guard and he had to admit, he had too. They had simply enjoyed each other, and the sweetness they made together.

Pulling on his pants, he walked to the door to another round of hard pounding. It was either an emergency or some other crisis.

Decker opened the door to his father's stormy face.

"You *are* in here with her." Russ brushed past Decker to enter the room. "What the hell are you doing?"

Decker let the hotel room door shut and went to where his father stood looking around the room. Did he really have to deal with this now? His father was acting like a five-year-old.

"I'm a grown man, Dad, not a young kid you can discipline anymore."

"So you did sleep with her."

Just then, Kendall appeared from the bedroom in a white robe, tying it tight around her waist.

"There she is, looking the part to boot," Russ said.

"Excuse me?" Kendall retorted.

This would spiral out of control—fast. Decker moved in front of his father so he stood between him and Kendall.

"Get rid of her, Decker."

"No. You're going to leave now," Decker said.

"I'm not leaving until you get rid of that trash. I will not have her in my hotel."

Kendall looked appalled, mouth dropping open and hand to her upper chest.

Decker felt like punching his father. "All right, you get out now!"

"I forbid you to marry this girl!"

"You're the one who picked her. It isn't my fault you didn't check her out beforehand to make sure she met your ridiculous standards!"

"Yes, and I own that mistake, now all I can do is damage control and that includes stopping you from making a colossal mistake yourself."

Frustration billowed up and nearly made Decker lose his composure. "I have done everything you asked or expected of me for years. Now when I go and do what I want, you climb all over me." Decker leaned close to his father and pointed his finger at his face. "You can't tell me what to do anymore. *I* decide what woman I see and *I* decide whether to marry her or not. Do you understand? I won't put up with these tirades anymore. If you ask me to choose between the decisions I make for myself and you, I'll choose my decisions." He lowered his hand.

Russ's face reddened. No one ever spoke to him this way, least of all Decker. "This is my company. I *can* and *will* tell you what to do with it."

"That doesn't include dictating who I can and cannot marry. If Kendall will have me, I intend to marry her at the end of this month."

The redness faded from Russ's face and he was speechless for several seconds. "You ungrateful brat. I've given you everything. You've had it handed to you with silver spoons and this is the thanks I get?"

"You didn't hand me the success to this lodge. You need me. No one else can run this company better than I can and you know it."

"If you marry that woman, I will not appoint you CEO of my company."

His father would never let go of control. Even if he did appoint Decker CEO, he'd still have his thumb on Decker at all times. Decker realized he could not live that way anymore. He knew his personal worth and he deserved more respect than that. What sickened him most was that Russ was his father, and his father treated his own son that way.

"Well, I am marrying her, so I'll save you the trouble. I quit." Decker turned and walked toward Kendall. "Let's get dressed and get out of here."

"What do you mean you *quit*? You can't *quit*," Russ said, still ranting. "You're just saying that. You won't leave this company. You don't have it in you. It means as much to you as it does me."

Decker turned at the bedroom door. "Really. I never would have known you thought that way given the way you treat me. I'm done, Dad. Unless you can pull your head out of your ass and prove you can be sensible, I will not be coming back."

"I'll cut you out of my will, Decker!" Russ roared.

"Fine. I have my own money." He slammed the bedroom door shut and dressed while Kendall packed her things.

"I can't believe you just did that," she said as she worked.

"Well, believe it. I should have done it sooner."

"I don't want you to quit because of me."

He walked over to the side of the bed where she filled a suitcase. "It isn't about you. My father has been ordering me around and hanging ultimatums over my head ever since I started working here. I let it pass because the lodge means so much to me and I wanted to succeed." He exhaled roughly. "But now I realize succeeding can't come with the price of compromising who I am to achieve it. And my father needs to understand that. He won't unless I leave and he sees the gaping hole that will be left in my absence."

"I hope you're right."

"I am." He leaned closer and kissed her. "Because of you."

"Me?" She searched his eyes.

"Yes, you. You're an amazing woman, Kendall. It doesn't matter if your family is in financial trouble. That doesn't change the woman you are. I'm embarrassed for my father. He has no right to judge you or talk about you the way he does. It makes him arrogant and superficial."

She smiled warmly and placed her hand on the side of his face. "You're an amazing man, Decker. And you're nothing like your father."

"That's reassuring." He grinned and she laughed lightly.

When they were ready to go, Decker left the room before her, seeing his father still there. The man had no conscience.

"So, you're really going to do this," Russ said.

"We're leaving now. Don't talk to me unless you can be civil." He stopped in front of Russ. "And if you talk about Kendall the way you did this morning ever again, I'll beat you."

Some of the haughtiness left Russ's eyes. "What's gotten into you?"

"A breath of fresh air." He reached for Kendall's hand and saw her meet Russ's look with defiance.

"You'll be back in the morning," Russ called after them.

"I won't ever be back, Dad, not if I have to work for a tyrant like you." He helped Kendall with her luggage, pulling it for her to the elevator.

Russ trailed behind them. "I'm your father!"

"Much to my embarrassment right now." Decker faced him from the elevator.

Russ had stopped in the hall and didn't get on with them.

Decker put his arm around Kendall, making it clear where his loyalty lay. Russ took note of it with considerable shock. He seemed to grapple with this drastic change in Decker. Hopefully he'd realize he was the one making the mistake, not Decker.

The elevator door closed.

Another snowstorm descended that afternoon, but that didn't stop Trey from arranging a meeting. Kendall watched it snow while everyone got settled and servants passed out beverages. Decker had insisted on having this meeting at his house because his security was good and Kendall wouldn't have to venture out into the dangers of the city. Trey had talked with the contractor who'd referred Emilio to her father.

She faced the living room. Decker stood with Trey as the two of them talked. Her parents sat together on the sofa, also talking.

"Thanks for coming out here," Decker said to Trey.

Not feeling like sitting, Kendall folded her arms.

Decker came to stand beside her, slipping his arms around her in show of comfort and support. Her parents quieted and looked to Trey, who stood in front of the fireplace.

"We've made what I call progress on the Elardi case," Trey said, looking dapper in a tan jacket, a white shirt and blue jeans. "I managed to locate the contractor

Bernard reported referred him to Elardi. His name is Antonio Garcia and he does single-family homes for developments. He was surprised when we showed up on his current job, but cooperative. He said he heard about the ransom victim but didn't believe Emilio was responsible. When we went over the evidence, he changed his mind."

"Was he telling you the truth?" Kendall asked. Antonio could be as crooked at Emilio. "He didn't know?"

"Emilio paid him a commission for every referral. According to Antonio, they never talked about them afterward. Antonio would send him referrals, Emilio would pay him and that was the extent of their dealings."

"Did Emilio specify any criteria for Antonio?" Decker asked.

"He did," Trey said. "He wanted clients who had nowhere else to turn."

And Antonio hadn't at least thought that was suspicious? "How do they know each other?" Kendall asked her father.

"I don't know. He never said."

"I asked Antonio that question and he said he built a guest house for him and does other odd jobs for him. He didn't indicate he knew what kind of man Elardi was."

"So he's on the up-and-up?" Bernard asked.

"I'm not sure. I find it odd that he'd take money from a man like Emilio and not know or even suspect that the ransom story was connected to him. He referred the father of the kidnapped victim," Trey said.

Antonio had to have at least suspected Emilio's involvement. Had he turned a blind eye to keep the money rolling in?

"Antonio willingly provided copies of the deposits he made after Emilio paid him. It's substantial enough to give him motive to keep quiet. And we don't know whether Emilio threatened him in any way. I asked and Antonio denied being threatened."

"I'd be afraid of someone like Emilio too," Kendall said. She *was* afraid of him.

"There's more," Trey continued. "We tapped Antonio and had him tailed. He met with Emilio after being questioned by us. During the course of their discussion it came out that Emilio hired a gunman to kidnap Kendall."

Kendall sucked in air. Although she had suspected something like this, having it confirmed shocked her. Her father had done business with a man who paid someone to kidnap her and likely murder her to keep her from identifying anyone involved.

She glanced at Decker and saw his jaw working, a clear indicator that he was angry with the news.

Her mother bent her head and began to cry. When Bernard tried to put his arm around her, she shrugged him off and stood. Kendall went to her and took her in for an embrace. Over her shoulder she could see her father looking on, a beaten man.

"We got the name of the gunman," Trey went on to say, turning to Decker after her mother calmed a bit. "He's got a record."

Trey brought over a photograph.

Kendall moved away from her mother to take it from him. She looked at a man with thick black hair and dark eyes.

"This is the man Emilio hired," Trey said.

Decker moved so he could see the photo as well. His nearness warmed her as frequently happened.

The man had the same build as the one she'd seen in the car, but she hadn't gotten a good enough look at him to be certain this was the same person.

"Do you recognize him?" Decker asked.

She shook her head. "I never got a close look at him. This man has the same body type but that's all I can tell you. That and he has shoulder-length dark hair, like this man." She looked at Trey. "How tall is he?"

"Six-one."

She nodded. "It could definitely be him, but he always wore sunglasses. I'm not sure I could pick him out in a lineup."

"This is enough for now. We'll keep looking for him."

Kendall was immensely relieved that they at least had identified her attacker. With any luck, they'd catch him before he struck again.

Two days later, Decker received a call from his father. He knew what this would entail before he answered. His dad had been out of The Lodge's general operations for some time now. He had no doubt run into problems only Decker could resolve.

"Hello," he said into the cell phone.

"Hi, son," his father humbly said. "We need to talk. Can you come and meet me?"

Decker looked over at Kendall, who waited at the front door. He was supposed to take her to work so she could meet with her wildlife biologist and his team to discuss her wolves. She wouldn't go alone after the bombing.

"What about? I have plans," Decker said, but he felt the familiar pull of ambition running The Lodge always gave him.

"I need you. There are multiple issues going on here."

Decker didn't respond as he silently analyzed his options.

"Please," Russ said. "I know I was out-of-bounds the last time we talked."

Talked? Argued and fought more described that. "You were *way* out of bounds."

"When can you be here?" his dad asked without acknowledging Decker's comment.

"I have to take Kendall to Hadley Forestry. I can come by after five."

"That will be too late. One of the lifts isn't working and I'm having trouble with the agreement with the vendor."

A ski lift not working meant skiers were not getting to their slopes. Major issue. Decker felt the pull intensify. The Lodge really needed him. Now.

"Decker?" his dad said after several moments of silence.

"Yes?"

"We need to talk anyway. Please come back."

"All right. I'm on my way." He didn't wait for his dad to end the call. He ended the call himself and looked at Kendall.

Already he could see her disappointment. She'd angled her head slightly and stuck one foot out, hitching a hip in what he could only call annoyance.

"A ski lift stopped working and my dad can't fix it.

People are waiting in lines." How could he make her understand the dire urgency of this situation? Decker already suffered the impacts of the Rouge murder. And his passion for the care and feeding of The Lodge was tantamount to the whole notion of true love.

"I can go myself to my meeting," Kendall said.

He heard the halfhearted tone and knew she did not want to go alone.

He went to her. Standing a foot or so from her, he took her hands in his. "Darling, I know how much those wolves mean to you, but can you reschedule your meeting?"

"Ben can't meet any other day this week. He drove all the way from Lakewood, which is basically Denver. So, no, I can't reschedule."

"I've got to go meet my dad. He's going to ruin everything I've built at The Lodge."

"I understand that."

Hearing her tone again, he did not believe her. But he'd made up his mind.

"I have to go. I'm sorry. Not only do I need to address some serious issues, exactly what I'd hoped would happen is coming to pass. My father is realizing how much he needs me." This was why an arranged marriage appealed to him so much. He needed a woman who would understand when issues like this came up and he had to drop everything to attend to them. He'd always be there for her but she had to allow him the freedom to work. And once her attacker was captured, this wouldn't be a problem.

He felt her weigh his issue versus hers. His business versus hers.

She became eerily calm and unreadable. She straightened and looked at him as though he were one of his business associates.

"Go ahead," she said, walking back into the house.

Decker experienced a moment of guilt. His gut told him not to go meet his dad, but if he didn't he'd be set back too much to possibly recover. He could put off his father, but not the business. And to Kendall's benefit, if The Lodge did well, so would her family's company.

Putting his business first over her wolves would hurt their relationship. He knew that. But his hands were tied here.

"Kendall…"

"Just go."

With his gut churning with the wrongness of it, he didn't stay.

Feeling as though he had betrayed Kendall gnawed at Decker's conscience as he made his way to his father's office. His head spun with how much she affected him. How much she made him feel. He grappled with the foreign emotion. He had never felt this way before.

Since when did he feel bad about putting his business first?

He reached his father's office, pausing at the door to attempt to shake himself into focus before entering. Russ looked up from his computer and relief washed over his expression. He stood.

"Thank you for coming, Decker." Russ walked around his desk.

"I haven't agreed to come back to work yet." Decker had to stand firm on his principles.

Russ put his hand on Decker's back. "I know. I've prepared for that. Let's go over here to the table."

Decker went there, seeing papers set out.

"I've appointed you CEO. All you have to do is sign. Have your lawyer look it over if you want. You don't have to sign today."

Decker looked at his father in surprise. This he had not expected. A true dangling carrot. Russ must really want him back or he wouldn't have gone this far. But Decker needed him to accept Kendall.

"What about Kendall?" Decker asked.

"I told you I was out of bounds."

"That isn't good enough. How can I be sure you won't treat her like a lesser being because of her father's mistakes?"

"I won't. I give you my word. My love of this company sometimes makes me lose touch with the rest of the world. I am protective of its success. The Hadleys' financial trouble made me panic."

Decker could understand that. He also appreciated his father's sincere candor. He rarely apologized, but Decker could see he truly meant it.

"I'm not unreasonable," Russ said. "I just lost control because I was afraid of what the Hadleys would do to The Colton Empire. I see now that your marriage to Kendall wouldn't jeopardize that. You wouldn't do anything to threaten the livelihood we've worked so hard to build."

"I do intend on looking into investing in Hadley Forestry. I am very interested in taking on the challenge of turning the business around." His father had to understand where he stood before he made him CEO of his precious company.

Russ's face pinched a little. He clearly did not like hearing that.

"Do you trust me?" Decker asked.

Russ blinked once. "Yes, son, I do. I only worry you'd invest for Kendall and not based on good business sense."

"It would be both, Dad. But I wouldn't try to save something that isn't salvageable. I haven't seen the books yet."

After a moment, Russ nodded. "Fair enough." He extended his arm to the table. "How about signing so you can get to work fixing all the bugs that infected this place since you left."

After Kendall had phoned Ben, he'd offered to come to her. They'd met at Decker's house. The wolves were thriving and would likely have a litter soon. Ben decided not to put a tracker on any of them, leaning more toward letting them live untouched by humans. He'd check on them on a regular basis but not so often as to scare them off.

Now in a nightgown and watching a movie, she yawned. Decker still wasn't home and it was after nine. He hadn't even called her.

She tried not to let that get to her, but the letdown wormed its way in anyway. This is why he pushed for marriage with her. He thought she'd be okay with being kicked to the curb so he could give all his energy to The

Lodge. She hadn't thought it would bother her since she wasn't interested in getting hurt again. But more and more she felt she'd be hurt no matter how hard she tried to avoid it.

Nevertheless, she hadn't changed her mind about marrying Decker. And she wouldn't unless her instinct told her she would be all right, that she wouldn't be hurt, and as of this moment, her instinct said the opposite. She felt as though she would be hurt, because she could fall in love with him and what if he never returned that love?

Hearing the front door open, she looked back over her shoulder and saw him remove his jacket as he stepped into the living room. Draping that over the back of a chair, he moved closer.

"Hi," he said in a deep, raspy voice she wished didn't make her tingle.

"Busy day?" She faced the television.

"A lot of problems." He came to sit beside her. "Kendall, I'm really sorry about leaving you the way I did."

She waved her hand in dismissal. "It's done. Ben came here for our meeting. How did it go with your dad?"

"He made me CEO. He also apologized."

She looked at him.

"He admitted his love for his company sometimes clouds his judgment."

"But he'll always look at me like you married a poor person, or someone beneath him," she said, her temper rising as it had when Russ had insulted her. Who did he think he was? Money didn't make a person better than anyone else. Russ was greedy that's all. And that would never change, no matter what Decker believed.

"No he won't. Especially not after I improve revenue at Hadley Forestry," he said.

"You plan on doing that?"

"Yes. I'd like to talk to your dad."

She nodded. "Okay. Let's go in the morning."

"I've got to go to The Lodge tomorrow."

Kendall felt the same sting she'd felt when he'd abandoned her this morning. She looked away from him.

How could he so easily turn his back on her? And why did she feel like he was anyway? He had to go to work. Investing in Hadley Forestry would be work too. Why did he have to put it second?

She may be overreacting but she couldn't help it. "I'm going to sleep." She stood. "In the guest room."

"Kendall." He stood with her.

"Good night, Decker." She left the living room, hoping he wouldn't follow her and try to smooth things over. He didn't.

She needed this night alone. Things had gone so well over the last couple of days. Now she felt she'd gotten another man wrong again. She'd thought Decker would work out for her, but she no longer did. He'd end up being another mistake.

Chapter 13

Kendall woke the next morning, groggily reaching over for Decker. She'd just had the best dream about him. Not feeling him beside her, she lifted her head and clarity returned. She'd slept in the guest room. Decker was probably already gone.

Getting up, she took her time showering, wondering what she'd do to fill her day. With her attacker still free, she didn't feel safe leaving, and there were plenty of ways to entertain herself at Decker's house. She could work out. She could watch a movie. She could read in his fabulous library. She could also invite her mother over for lunch. Maybe her friends.

The rare warm days this time of year had cooled. Finished dressing in jeans and a sweatshirt, she left the room and made her way downstairs. In the kitchen, she saw coffee had been made. She poured a cup and went to sit at the dining table, turning on the television to catch up on the news.

Hearing the front door open, she saw Decker carrying a big vase of flowers.

"You're up," he said. "My surprise for you is ruined."

"Contraire," she said. "I am surprised. I thought you'd be at work by now."

He came to the kitchen and set the vase down, leaning toward her and planting a kiss on her lips. "I want to take you with me."

To work? With him? His cologne distracted her along with his warm breath and brown eyes smoldering into hers.

"I promised you a tour," he said. "You haven't had one yet."

"I've seen most of it already." She admired the array of pretty spring flowers and smelled the lilies.

"Not all of it," Decker said. "Come with me."

It was either that or stay here and be lonely. "All right."

Kendall didn't want to appear easily swayed, but spending the day with Decker excited her. She just had to remind herself that he was a savvy businessman who wasn't accustomed to losing. He'd fight hard to win her over and his invitation to go with him to work had to be another attempt to secure her.

He had his driver take them to work and used his cell to tell his assistant that he'd be delayed for at least two hours and to call if anything important came up.

"You ready for a long walk?" he asked her.

"Oh yeah." She missed hiking in the wilderness. This

wasn't exactly rugged terrain, built up into a fancy resort, but it would do. So would Decker's undivided attention.

He began with a walk to the original hotel.

"Employees who don't want to commute live here now," he said.

She took in the historic architecture that had been meticulously updated and maintained. If she worked here she'd love to live in a place like this.

"Pine Peak has an ample amount of slopes for skiing but we also offer areas for extreme winter sports," he said.

First he took her by the luxurious cabins tucked away in trees, very private and away from most activities. Next, he had a snowmobile ready for them. Kendall climbed on the back and slipped her arms around him as he began driving.

Near the ski slopes, Decker stopped the snowmobile at the entrance to a track. Getting off, she walked with him to the entrance, seeing bleachers for viewing and a few people riding snow bikes around an obstacle course, as well as a racetrack with banks, turns and jumps. They went to the bleachers and watched for a while. Kendall didn't care much for races like this but she could see Decker's enjoyment.

"These were my idea," he said, "to add extreme sporting events." Looking over at her and likely seeing that she didn't share his enthusiasm, he said, "All right, next stop."

Taking her hand he walked with her to the snowmobile. She climbed on again, liking the feel of her arms around him and being so close. She wondered if he felt the same.

He drove the snowmobile fast along a trail. Around a bend, she spotted another track, this one a steep slope sparkling in the sun. It was a sheet of ice and people were racing down in boatlike structures.

"Are those kayaks?" she asked.

He slowed the snowmobile and stopped at the side of the slope. "They sure are. It's getting to be a popular sport."

"Crazy!" She watched one kayak boater lose control and crash into deeper snow on the other side of the slope.

"Do you want to give it a try?" he asked.

"No way!" Was he kidding? After seeing someone crash?

He chuckled and she realized he had been joking. She gave him a swat as he got the snowmobile moving again. Back on the trail, he followed it to a ski lift. Skiers lined up for their day of fun.

He took her to the worker at the chairlift, who immediately recognized him and let them take the next chair. She warmed sitting close beside him, their legs touching. When she glanced at him she saw his pleasure in sharing something he cared so much about, which soon morphed into heated desire.

As his gaze lingered, Decker put his gloved fingers beneath her chin and kissed her deeply. Kendall fell into the warm caress. At last when he drew back, she then fell into the sincere emotion she saw in him. She could not be mistaken. He felt something for her. Why didn't he admit it?

Suddenly he looked away. "We almost missed it."

She looked where he did and saw three kite skiers.

They held on to their chute-like kites and snowboarded over a gently sloping field of snow. It was beautiful. The skiers were clearly experienced and made a sort of ballet as they glided along.

"You see? There is much more to this lodge than elegant dinners and famous guests," he said.

"Yes, I see that," she answered. "I also see how proud you are of this place, and rightfully so."

"Thank you. Coming from you that means a lot."

She raised a curious brow. "Why me?"

"Because I don't want you to think I put The Lodge before you, or anyone that is close to me. This lodge is a very close second, though."

She smiled, hearing and feeling his honesty. "I understand." Whether she could live with that was another matter. She decided it was time to test him.

Decker floated in the clouds, so happy to hear Kendall come in line with his purpose and where she fit into that. They rode the chair without getting off, heading back to the base.

"Decker?"

"Yes?"

"I think I love you," she said in a low voice.

Unprepared for the abruptness of that announcement, he first wondered why she'd said it. Why now?

She hadn't said she loved him. She'd said she *thought* she loved him. That's the thing about being in love. Nobody ever really knew if they were or not.

"You just like me a lot," he said lightly.

"No. I really do think I love you."

He stared at her. "What makes you say that?"

She put her hand on his thigh and caressed. After a few seconds, she looked into his eyes.

"The way I feel when we're together," she whispered. "I can't get enough of you. It's like you take the air I breathe. And…when you leave me it stings."

"When I go to work?" She had just told him she understood.

"No, when you leave me even though we have plans."

"This is about Ben?" Why had she started out by saying she loved him?

"No. This is about me being scared, Decker. I love you and you don't love me. It's like my live-in boyfriend all over again."

Ah, so this was about her insecurity. "This is not the same, Kendall. I will never betray you. I will always be here for you and we will always have this intimate companionship."

She put her head against his shoulder with a contented sigh. "You talk as though we'll be together for a lifetime."

"We will be."

She lifted her head. "Only if I marry you."

"You will." He grinned to keep it light.

She didn't respond, her expression serious as she met his eyes. Wow. She sure was stubborn. She would not marry him unless she was certain it was right for her.

"What do you need from me to agree to this marriage?" he asked.

"An honest proposal."

Chapter 14

Back at the lodge, Kendall hadn't decided whether she'd triggered Decker to begin thinking about love. Telling him she loved him had stunned him, which might be a good sign. He'd have a lot to consider now, namely his belief that love didn't happen to people like him. Maybe he'd reevaluate how he felt and realize what they had together wasn't ordinary.

"Decker."

Kendall turned with Decker to see Decker's cousin Remy Colton coming toward them. She had heard he was The Chateau's director of public relations. Tall with wavy light brown hair, he wore an immaculately pressed three-piece suit.

"There you are," Remy said as he came to a stop.

"Sorry I'm late." Decker shook Remy's hand and

leaned in for a man hug, which was little more than a couple of pats.

"What did you want to meet about?" Remy asked.

"You're good at public relations," Decker answered. "We're having a public relations crisis here with the Rouge murder. I'd like to discuss ideas on boosting business."

"I'd be happy to. But if now isn't a good time we can reschedule. You seem busy today."

Decker glanced at Kendall with a secretive grin. She had been what had kept him busy.

"No, now is good."

Remy caught the exchange, Kendall noted, his observant gaze going from Decker to her.

Apparently not noticing, Decker said to her, "Kendall, you might as well join us."

He turned to the reception desk where a receptionist stood with Remy's half brother, Seth, who at the moment was giving her a pep talk on how to talk to difficult customers. The young woman was slim, neatly dressed in a short-sleeved black dress. She listened and nodded, but Kendall sensed she didn't appreciate Seth's tutelage.

"Can you check to see if the conference room is open up here?" Decker asked.

"Yes." Seth showed the receptionist, who must be new, how to look up the availability of the room. While she checked, Seth turned to Decker and Remy. "What are you meeting about?" Kendall thought that was an odd question. He was the front desk manager. Was he always this curious?

Decker glanced at her and seemed to see her notice.

"Seth and Remy are half brothers," Decker said.

"When I was fifteen, he found me living with our mother, who had a problem with drugs." Seth smiled at Remy, who looked on with reciprocating affection.

"Ah." That made sense to Kendall. "I see."

"We are meeting about public relations," Decker said to Seth. "The Rouge murder has impacted our reservations. I'd like to get his take on strategy, and maybe discuss what he's done at The Chateau."

"I have an idea I'd like to share," Seth said. "Would you mind?"

That explained his curiosity.

"I'm all ears," Decker said.

Kendall was sure he would be open to any suggestions. If she were someone who planned to stay at a resort like this, she didn't think a murder—which hadn't even occurred here—would scare her away. The call girl had only stayed here. Then again, some people might be sensitive to that, especially wealthy people. The hotel was now tainted with the reputation of allowing prostitution on its premises.

"Car washes are always fun," Seth said.

Kendall watched him lift a hand, a somewhat dainty move.

"You know, with all those girls in swimming suits, laughing and giggling and taking money from all the men?" he added.

Kendall looked at Decker to see if he thought that suggestion was as horrible as she did. He just stared at Seth.

"It's still March," Remy said.

"I didn't mean now, after it warms up," Seth clarified.

"We need to act now," Decker said. "We don't have time to spare. Reservations are down, as I'm sure you're aware."

"Yes, sir. That's why I'm so interested in helping find a solution."

"Well, keep trying and let me know if you come up with any others."

Seth beamed. "Thank you. I will."

"I appreciate your enthusiasm." With that, Decker walked away with Remy.

Kendall saw Seth still smiling as they left and then she followed Decker.

Decker let Kendall into the room and then closed the conference area door behind them and sat beside Kendall, across from Remy.

"What was he thinking?" Remy asked with a dry chuckle.

"Or *not* thinking," Decker said.

"Well, it would draw attention but not the right kind for your clientele," Kendall added.

"It might promote more call girls," Decker mused, and they laughed at the dark humor.

"Rich people have skeletons of that nature in their closets just like anyone else," Remy said. "Bianca coming to see one of your guests proves that."

Kendall saw Decker sober. "Exactly why we're meeting today."

"Yes." Remy fell in line in sobriety.

"Seth is a good front desk manager. People like him even though he is a little eccentric," Decker said.

"He is a good kid," Remy said proudly. "But he may as well have come up with the idea of a crossword puzzle party."

Again they chuckled, the mood lightening.

"I've actually been thinking about some ideas as well," Kendall said. "My conservancy work is along the same lines, where I look for ways to preserve the wilderness. More human activities isn't preservation. You're looking for ways to preserve the reservations of your elite guests."

Decker's eyes heated with intimate appreciation.

"Do tell," Remy said.

"What about a charity event for an organization like Change for Life. They help victims of human trafficking begin new lives free from their captors. It would show you care about ethics and in particular, sex trafficking."

Decker didn't say anything for a while. "Is that related to forced prostitution?"

Yes," Remy said."

"We also don't want to appear too desperate to remove the stigma of a high-class call girl being murdered after visiting one of our guests," Decker added.

"I'll get my marketing team right on this," Remy said. "We'll make it an exceptionally elegant event."

"Speaking of elegant events, are you going to Bree's opening?" Decker asked. Their talented artist cousin ran Wise Gal gallery.

"Yes, I'll be there, as I'm sure many others in the family will be,"

Decker glanced at Kendall. "Will you accompany me?"

"Sounds lovely. Yes."

"It will be an official date."

"Haven't our other dates been official?" she asked.

"No, because that was when we were doing it for our parents. Now I want us to date for real."

She smiled, unable to stop herself and knowing she must appear as smitten as she felt.

"I feel like I'm intruding," Remy deadpanned. "How's the investigation going? I heard you've had some close calls lately."

He'd steered the talk away from dating. Kendall found that amusing.

"Yes," Decker answered. "Trey may have ID'd the suspect. Kendall couldn't be sure it was him."

"Well, I hope they catch him soon. Scary knowing he's out there."

Yes, and planning ways to get to her, no doubt. She looked at Decker. At least she had him to protect her.

He met her look and she fell into another long gaze with him.

"Looks like your wedding plans are going forward," Remy said. "Arranged marriages do work out sometimes, judging by the two of you."

"I'm happy to agree," Decker replied.

Kendall remained silent. She wasn't ready to commit to that.

"Kendall is still altar shy," Decker said, "But I'm working on that."

"So the date is a ploy?" Kendall asked, teasing.

"No, more of a strategy."

Remy laughed briefly. "You better watch out, Kendall. Once my cousin sets his eyes on something nothing will stop him from winning. He's very decisive in business."

In business. Of course. But this was personal.

Decker stepped into the Wise Gal Gallery on Second Street in Roaring Springs, on the edge of an up-to-the-minute part of town. An older two-story warehouse renovated into this stylish art gallery, the Wise Gal had charm all its own. Inside, people mingled and held champagne glasses. A wide, open space with white walls, statues were arranged here and there and paintings hung on the walls.

"Did your cousin do all of these?" Kendall asked.

"Bree sells other art along with her own. Hers are over there in that corner." He once again admired Kendall in that sleeveless white cocktail dress that flattered her tall, graceful form and flared at the knee. He had on a dark suit and tie.

She finished looking at the assortment of trendy art, some abstract, some landscape. "She's quite good."

"She's always been very artistic." He put his hand on her lower back as they walked farther into the gallery.

"And this building is so nice."

"Yes. She lives upstairs." Decker spotted his parents, and across the room stood Bernard and Marion. He saw how Russ sent occasional disapproving glares their way. He probably didn't think they belonged at this elegant affair.

Decker recognized a lot of Coltons in attendance.

He and Kendall had arrived late by design. Everyone was here.

Phoebe and Skye Colton stood next to each other; Decker could barely tell the identical twins apart. Each thin but curvy with long red hair, their personalities were the main differentiator. Skye's animated way of communicating gave her away. Phoebe was the quieter of the two.

Trey Colton had stopped to talk with the mayor. He wore his cowboy hat even at this event.

Colton cousin Mason Gilford stood with his wife, Elaine, as they admired a painting. Director of sales for The Colton Empire, it was rumored he held some bitterness over the Coltons' legacy. Decker had also heard the couple was trying to have a baby. It was difficult to avoid hearing gossip in this town.

At last he found the host. Bree talked with some people he didn't recognize. In a silky gold-and-black floral dress with a fitted bodice, high waist and a flared, wrap skirt, she looked stunning and artsy.

"There's Bree." Decker pointed her out to Kendall.

Bree saw him and smiled with a graceful wave. Saying something to the couple she'd been engaged with, she headed over to them.

"She looks like Antonia Thomas," Kendall commented, admiring her light brown complexion and warm, golden brown eyes.

Bree reached them and gave Decker a hug.

"Congratulations on your art opening, cuz."

"Thanks, Decker." She stepped back and smiled at Kendall. "You must be the lovely fiancée I've been hearing so much about." Bree leaned toward her and gave her a noninvasive hug.

"Hi."

Talk must have really spread about their upcoming marriage.

"Your paintings are amazing," Kendall said.

"Oh, thank you." Bree glanced over at her display. "Art means everything to me."

"It shows," Decker said. He looked around. "The place looks great."

"Yes, I'm so happy the way it turned out. I'm so fortunate to have come this far so soon."

"Hard work and dedication pay off," Decker said. "You most definitely have that."

"Oh, and you don't, Mr. Rock-Star Lodge Operator."

Decker smiled without comment.

Someone came up to Bree and asked about one of her paintings.

"Would you excuse me?" she said to Decker and Kendall.

"Of course," Kendall said.

Bree headed over to her display with the guest and they began conversing about one of the paintings.

"She seems so sophisticated."

"She's a good person. Built all of this on her own," Decker said. "She made money on her paintings and used that to invest in this building. Got a really good price on it."

Kendall started walking toward her parents and he joined her. She hugged her mother.

"I didn't know you two were planning on being here," she said.

"You know how your mother loves art," her dad replied. "Decker, how are you?"

"Fine. You?"

"Getting by."

"How are you really, Kendall?" her mother asked.

"I'm fine, mother. Decker is taking care of me." She meant as far as protection but it may have come out wrong.

"Is the wedding still on?"

Decker watched Kendall's face stiffen. Had Bernard asked in the hopes Decker would bail him out? Decker didn't blame her for being offended.

"Yes," Decker said anyway.

"We're talking about it," Kendall corrected.

Well, he had every intention of sealing the deal. And soon. He still had to come up with a creative way of proposing to her.

Bernard's face sagged a little. Clearly he was disappointed to hear there may not be a wedding.

"Kendall."

She turned with Decker to see Russ standing there.

She moved to open the circle more, a welcoming gesture given how rude Decker's father had been to her.

"I'd like to apologize for the way I spoke to you."

"Thank you, Mr. Colton."

"Did I hear correctly that you may not marry my son?" he asked.

"Yes. I haven't decided."

"We're hoping she does," Bernard said.

"I'll bet you are," Russ retorted rather caustically.

"Dad," Decker cautioned.

Russ raised a hand in surrender. "I trust your choices, son. Just don't do anything rash from a business perspective, that's all I ask."

By that he must mean invest in Hadley Forestry if their numbers were as bad as suspected.

"Champagne?" he asked Kendall.

"Yes."

He walked with her to the bar that had been set up and they each took a glass from the bartender. Moving over to stand in the front corner, he observed the crowd with her. Art shows weren't really his thing but he enjoyed the social interaction.

A loud crash preceded something hard and heavy flying through the air. Before Decker could react, a brick tumbled to the floor and shards of glass sprinkled him and Kendall. A larger one struck Kendall's face.

She gave a shriek and fell into him. He caught her and eased her down, seeing she was hit near her right eye—too near. Blood ran down her face.

"Somebody call 911!" he shouted, and then searched for something to put on her wound. Someone handed him a wad of napkins and he pressed that to her face.

He saw Trey run out the front, presumably to chase whoever had thrown a brick through the gallery window.

"Decker?"

"I'm here, darling. Just stay still. Paramedics are on their way."

"Is it bad?"

He couldn't tell with all the blood. "You'll be all right."

"I can't see out of my right eye and I'm dizzy like I'm going to pass out."

She frightened him when she said that. How hard had she been hit? "You can't see because of the bleeding. Try to stay calm."

Bree had rushed over and now knelt beside Kendall. "Oh my gosh, what happened?"

"Someone threw a brick through your front window," Decker said. "Glass hit Kendall and cut her face."

"Oh, no. Kendall, I'm so sorry. I'll pay for your medical expenses of course."

"No. Don't worry about that."

"Any sign of that ambulance?" Decker called out to anyone who could check outside. It had only been a minute or two but he was frantic to get her to the hospital. He did not like the look of her eye.

"Not yet," someone called.

Trey appeared, slowing from a run. "Is she all right?"

"She was cut by broken glass," someone said.

"Whoever threw it was gone when I got outside," Trey said.

Bree looked up at Trey with apprehension marring her face.

"Who would do that?" Trey barked.

She bit her lower lip.

"You know?"

"No, I don't know." Bree stood and faced Trey. "But I've been getting threats."

"What kind of threats?"

"Phone calls, mostly. Someone says I take advantage of people and need to be taught a lesson."

"Do you have any enemies? Anyone who might have a reason to do you harm?" Trey asked.

Bree shook her head. "I've tried to think of anyone who might do that but there isn't anyone."

"It could be racism," Trey said. "Even though you're half white, maybe someone is targeting you for being black."

"I suppose that's possible. Something random makes sense," she said.

The sound of sirens parted the crowd to make room for paramedics. Decker could only stand by helplessly as they worked over her, then put her on the gurney and wheeled her to the ambulance.

He climbed inside with her.

"Decker?" she said.

"I'm right here, my darling. I won't leave your side." He took her hand, gravely concerned for the condition of her eye.

Kendall woke some time later in a hospital bed. Doctors had done surgery on her face, telling her that the glass had cut her close to her eye. They hadn't been sure how much damage had been caused to the eye itself.

"Kendall?"

Hearing Decker's voice reassured her and calmed her. He pressed a tender kiss to her mouth.

She reached up and felt the bandage over her eye. "My eye."

"The doctor said your eye will be fine but you'll have to undergo plastic surgery to remove scarring."

She could do that. Kendall breathed in relief.

He took her hand and kissed her again. "You gave me quite a scare, darling."

"I was scared too."

"I'm so glad you're going to be all right."

"That makes two of us." She smiled and he chuckled. "Does this mean you love me now?"

She had to bring that up now? Was she teasing? Or testing him?

"I love being with you."

Her smile faded but she kept a light spirit. "That's a good start."

Chapter 15

Kendall was released from the hospital the next day. The side of her face was sore and bandaged but she was grateful that her injuries were not more severe. Decker took her to his suite at The Lodge and despite her protests, carried her the entire way up to the top-floor rooms. He placed her on his massive bed and commanded her to get some rest. Then he arranged for some of his staff to check in on her, as well as putting round-the-clock security outside the door.

She spent the remainder of the day resting with the television on, but now she was ready to get out of bed. Standing, her face throbbed with the movement and she reconsidered getting up. Just then the door to the suite opened and she saw Decker coming toward her.

His footsteps quickened when he saw her. Her grimace must have shown. She put her hand on the tall post at the foot of the bed.

Decker reached her and put his arm around her waist. "Are you all right?"

The pain killers had her a little woozy. "Yes, just a little dizzy."

"Let's get you back to bed."

"I'm tired of being in bed. I'd love a bath."

"All right, I'll run one for you. How is your injury? Are you in any pain?"

"A little."

He put his free arm under her legs and laid her back on the bed. Then he kissed her briefly with a warm greeting in his eyes. "Hi."

His soft but deep, raspy voice stirred her desire for him. "Welcome home."

Maybe the painkillers made her a little mushier than she'd be otherwise.

His handsome grin only kept the attraction burning.

"Wait here," he said.

He went into the bathroom and she listened to him start a bath. A few minutes later, he returned and lifted her again.

Kendall felt deliciously pampered as he carried her to the bathroom. She smelled lavender before she saw he'd put bubbles into the water, not giving any indication that her proximity affected him.

"There's a bath bomb in there too," he said as he let her feet down onto the floor.

She undressed and Decker helped her into the water.

"Mmm." She leaned back and closed her eyes. "Were you always this attentive?"

"With women? No. With my work? Yes."

She smiled and then winced as the skin pinched and caused her pain.

"Sorry." He chuckled.

She opened her eyes to see him. He sat on a bench that was in the large bathroom, regarding her warmly as he did before they made love.

"What do you think would have happened if we had dated in high school?" she asked.

"We'd have hit it off and then broken up when we went to college. We would have needed to grow up some more. You would have been the one I never forgot."

He was already the one she had never forgot.

"We would have grown up and then we'd still be right here the way we are right now," Decker pointed out.

She had to agree. Their dating in high school wouldn't have changed Russ arranging their marriage. In fact, it might have bolstered his motives.

They talked for several more minutes about stories from high school and college. The talking made her feel closer to him. She felt she knew him more after they finished. He was so easy to talk to. Then the water began to cool.

"I'm ready to get out," she said.

He helped her up and gave her a towel. She dried off, self-conscious that she was naked. Their talking and her taking a bath with him in the room had heated the chemistry between them. She could see it in his eyes, warmer now and growing hotter.

She dropped the towel, not meaning to, and stood still, seeing him take in her body with growing hunger. He came toward her.

In his arms, she met his mouth and kissed him back. The contact quickly spiraled into more. He lifted her and carried her to the bed, where he gently placed her down before removing all his clothes, his movements urgent and rushed.

On top of her, he kissed her as though he could devour her. She answered with equal passion until her cut gave her a sting. She made a small sound.

"Sorry," Decker rasped.

"It's okay. Don't stop." She ran her hands along his muscular arms.

"I don't want to hurt you." He took her nipple into his mouth and flicked the tip with his tongue.

"That's not hurting me."

He chuckled in a deep voice.

She moved her hands up to his shoulders and into his hair as he paid loving attention to her other breast. Her knees were parted and he lay between them.

He moved down to her stomach, kissing his way lower. When he found her sweet spot, she clenched her fingers into his hair. Too much of that and she'd be spent far too soon.

Luckily he must have sensed that because he moved down her right thigh, to her knee then to her ankle and kissed her big toe, eyes raised to look at her teasingly.

She chuckled this time.

Grinning seductively, he shifted between her legs again, coming down to kiss her softly. That wasn't enough for her. He was being ultracareful so as not to cause her pain.

The more time Kendall spent with him, the more comfortable she became, the more he became her best friend and partner. She could say anything to him and never got tired of being with him. This joining felt like a celebration of that magic.

She slid her hands over his rear, feeling the taunt muscles and pulling him against her.

He took her hint and probed for her, entering with a few firm thrusts until he sank inside and filled her. As he began to move, she did the same, angling for that perfect contact.

As always, their fire burst into hotter flames and soon he was pumping, stimulating her to orgasm.

Afterward, she lay against him as she always did, basking in the aftermath.

"Do you think we would have done that when we were in high school?" he asked.

To which she had to smile again. "Yes, but it wouldn't have been this spectacular."

"It would have been awkward and unwieldy?"

"I don't know. How many girls did you sleep with in high school?"

He flashed her a devilish grin. "Not as many as you probably think. Two."

"Only two?"

"Yes. I was choosy. I did fantasize about getting you in the sack, though."

She rose up onto her elbow. "You did not!"

"Oh, yes I did. Many times. You might have ruined me for other girls."

"I fantasized about you too," Kendall confessed.

"I know you did."

She gave him a swat and then set all humor aside. "I'm glad we didn't hook up in high school. This is special. It might not have been as meaningful back then."

He sobered along with her but said nothing. Kendall knew what he was thinking. That this was special because it might be love. She could see him fight it.

Resting her head on his shoulder, she let his resistance go without confronting him, content with this marvelous moment and hoping he was one more step closer to letting go of old convictions.

Decker left Kendall sleeping and went to work for a little while. After that, he had planned a meeting with Elardi—a surprise meeting. He took three of his security guards with him, men who had military backgrounds who he paid very well. With rich and famous guests frequently staying at The Lodge, the money was well spent.

In a neighboring mountain town, Decker stepped up to the entrance of the Royal Haven Casino. A massive commercial structure constructed of red brick and trimmed in light-colored stone, the casino took up a block in the downtown area. Awnings shaded the first level and groups of tall and narrow windows lined the second.

Inside, it looked like a typical casino, with lights everywhere and dings going off. People sat at slot machines or at the bar. Decker searched for the way to the corporate offices, which most likely were on the second floor. He and his guards walked through the main area of the casino. Seeing wide stairs, he headed there. Two men in black suits stood at the top, one bald and as big as Dwayne Johnson and the other younger with a full head of blond hair. They both moved to block their way as they reached the last stair.

"I'm here to see Mr. Elardi regarding a business proposal," Decker said.

"Is he expecting you?"

"No, but he'll be interested in hearing what I have to say."

"Name?"

"Decker Colton."

"And your friends?"

"Security."

The bigger of the two looked over the three with Decker before giving a nod to his partner.

Several minutes later, the partner came back. "He'll see you. Follow me."

Decker followed the man down the wide, dim hall to a set of double doors at the end. There were also additional doors on each side but all were closed. Decker wondered if they were bedrooms or other accommodations. Maybe offices for Elardi's staff.

The blond man opened the doors and Decker entered to see Emilio Elardi sitting behind a dark wood desk and four burly, savage-looking men scattered about the huge office. Two sat on a sofa, one stood by the desk and the other leaned against a bar.

Elardi stood. "Mr. Colton." He moved around the desk and offered his hand.

So far so good. Decker shook his hand. "Thanks for seeing me."

"I've heard of you and your family," Elardi said. "What brings you here?"

"I'm looking into investing in Hadley Forestry and in talking with Bernard, it seems he's got a loan with you."

"Yes. He does." Elardi gave no indication that he had bullied Bernard. He seemed perfectly comfortable and as though he conducted legitimate business with the man.

"I'm here to negotiate a settlement," Decker said.

"The terms are clearly stated in the contract Bernard signed."

"I've read the contract. It didn't say anything about kidnapping for ransom if he didn't pay by the due date." Decker took a risk saying that, but he wasn't afraid. He dealt with powerful people all the time.

Elardi kept a bland expression as he contemplated Decker and his three guards.

"Of course it didn't," Elardi finally said. "Who would do such a thing?"

"You," Decker replied, equally bland.

"You have proof of this?"

"Not yet, but I will…unless you agree to my terms."

Elardi grinned but not with any real humor. "What are your terms?"

"Cut the interest in half and deduct the amount from the balance and remove the requirement for Hadley Forestry to provide you with free lumber in perpetuity."

Now Elardi chuckled. "That is a ludicrous proposal, Mr. Colton. Surely you cannot expect me to agree."

"I do. The police have identified the man you hired to attempt to kidnap Kendall. It's only a matter of time before he talks."

"I don't know what you are talking about. I didn't hire anyone to kidnap Bernard's daughter."

"You know his daughter?" Decker asked. "I didn't think you ever met her. She didn't know about you until recently."

"Bernard mentioned her."

"Did he now?" Decker had his doubts. "That's easily checked. My guess is you deliberately looked into Bernard's background to find out as much as you could about him and his family in case you needed any collateral to force payment from him."

"Bernard entered into our agreement freely. He understood the terms and agreed to them."

"Your terms are ridiculous," Decker said. "Agree to mine and I'll pay you right now, the entire balance."

"What do you get in return?"

"Either a share of the company or Bernard can pay me back."

"You haven't spoken with Bernard?" Elardi asked.

"No, not yet."

"Why not?"

Decker wasn't going to get into details. "I have my reasons."

"Could those reasons be related to Kendall? She's quite beautiful. I think I'd be tempted to help out her family too."

Why was Elardi playing games? He must know Kendall was living with him. He probably also knew they were planning to get married.

It was time to be blunt. "Mr. Elardi, if you think my family is without resources to take care of this situation, I would advise you to think again."

That gave Elardi pause. For the first time his expression wasn't so aloof, as though he second-guessed Decker as he must so many others.

"If you don't agree to my terms, I'll arrange to eliminate this problem another way," Decker said. "We know several very influential people who can make your life miserable without much effort at all."

Elardi took a step toward him. "You dare to come in here and threaten me?"

Two of Decker's guards moved to his side, the other still behind him.

Elardi's men to Decker's right reached into their jackets and the two on the sofa stood up. Elardi held up a hand, stopping them from drawing what must be guns.

"I'll give you twenty-four hours to think it over." With that, Decker turned, flanked by his guards, and left.

Kendall woke from a nap, feeling much better now. Her cut didn't hurt so much and she had more energy. Rolling over to get out of bed, she saw a red ribbon tied to the post at the foot of the bed. A yellow note was taped to the ribbon.

What the…

She swung her legs over the edge of the bed and stood to flip the note over.

When my father first came to me with the idea to marry you, I didn't believe I would.

What was Decker up to? She looked toward the open room door and spotted another note. Going there, she lifted that one.

I love the way you appreciate good food.

Smiling, stopping when her cut stung, she followed the ribbon out into the main living area. Seeing Decker sitting at the table before the windows, holding the other end of the ribbon, she smiled again, knowing what he was up to now.

She went to the third note near where the ribbon was tied to a lamp on a console table.

I loved the first time we made love.

She made it to the side of the sofa and read the next note, glancing at Decker, who watched her intently.

I love the connection that's formed between us.

The second-to-last note read, *You must feel it too.*

Yes, she did, but did he? The last note was near his hand that held the end of the ribbon.

First meeting his eyes, feeling warm and tingly all over, she asked, "How long have you been sitting there holding that ribbon?"

"About an hour."

She lifted the yellow note.

Last night convinced me more than ever that there is no other woman for me.

Last night had convinced her too.

"Will you marry me?" he asked.

He hadn't told her he loved her but love had been in every single one of his notes. He had trouble admitting he had strong feelings for her that could be love. She decided right then that he was worth risking the chance that he'd never tell her he loved her.

"Yes."

He grinned broader and stood, pulling her to him as he stood. Holding her against him, he kissed her. "That's good, darling, because the wedding is all planned and the invitations have already been sent out."

"How romantic," she said, equally sarcastic as he sounded.

"I meant every word on those notes."

"I know you did," she whispered, kissing him.

"You know I'm going to…" She pressed her mouth to him again, "do everything in my power…" She gave him another soft peck, making him pause, "to be the husband you deserve, right?"

She withdrew and took his face between her hands. "Yes, Decker, I do."

This time, he kissed her. Then he lifted her into his arms and carried her back to the bedroom.

She felt how he had let down his guard, felt him exposing his heart to her. She doubted he knew what he felt, understood its power. She only hoped that someday he would.

Chapter 16

The next day, Decker went to work consumed with thoughts of Kendall and their night together. He had felt something deep inside, something strong and gripping, for her. It disconcerted him so much that he couldn't wait to get to work to get his mind off her. Except that hadn't happened. She clung to him, wrapped around his heart and didn't let go.

At nine in the morning, he received a call from Elardi, who accepted his offer. Only marginally distracted from Kendall, Decker had gone back to the casino and they'd signed a new agreement, which voided out the one between Elardi and Bernard.

Now he arrived at Hadley Forestry for a meeting with Bernard to share the good news. He couldn't wait to get started on turning the company around, and he especially couldn't wait to get back to Kendall and tell her everything was going to be all right now.

Bernard came out of his office and shook Decker's hand. "I wasn't expecting you today. Where is Kendall? How is she?"

"She's doing better. She's back at The Lodge."

"What a relief. Come on into my office." Bernard led the way and then faced Decker.

"I had a meeting with Emilio Elardi," Decker said without preamble.

Bernard looked alarmed. "And you're still alive?"

"We came to an understanding."

"What kind of understanding?"

"I've paid your loan with him in full, with conditions," Decker answered. "He reduced the interest and removed the requirement to provide free lumber."

"How did you get him to agree to that?" Bernard lifted his hand with a wave. "Never mind. I don't want to know. I just want to thank you so much."

"My pleasure."

"Does this mean Kendall will be safe now?" Bernard asked.

"I would assume so." Unless the hitman decided to seek revenge. "We need to talk about my role in your company, Bernard. I'm very interested in coming to work for you."

"What role would you want? Chief operating officer?"

"No, CEO. I need to be able to make decisions without interference from you."

"You'd listen to my input, though, wouldn't you?"

"Of course, but I would need complete control of the business, at least until I straighten things out."

"What do you mean, complete control?"

"I just invested a lot of money in this company. I expect to have free rein to ensure I make a profit. Now, if you aren't comfortable with that, you can pay back the loan to me instead of Elardi. I don't want to force you into anything."

"I do appreciate that. If I opt to pay you the loan, will you still help me with my company?"

Decker was afraid he'd ask for that. But given the amount of money, he had to be certain all business decisions—especially financial and strategic—would be his and his alone. He didn't have to be an expert on lumber to know how to make a company successful. Besides, it wouldn't take him long to get up to speed.

"I'm afraid I have to ask you to choose between the two options."

Bernard's brow shot low. "I either hand you over controlling interest or pay you the money back?"

"Yes."

"I wouldn't interfere, Decker. I'd give you free rein as long as I agree with your decisions."

Decker sighed. "That's the problem. If I make a decision I believe will help this company, then you have to let me."

"If you're sure it will, I won't interfere. You have my word."

His word wasn't good enough. As a businessman, Decker never gave favors to friends or family. He didn't know Bernard enough, least of all how he ran a business, so he'd be even less inclined to trust him.

"I'm sorry. Given the amount of money I just invested, I have to have something in writing."

Bernard's faced pinched slightly with anger. "Is my daughter going to marry you?"

"Yes. I proposed and she accepted."

"Then you leave me no choice. I'll have my lawyers draw something up."

Decker arrived back at The Lodge and found Kendall dressed in jeans and a sweater, reclined on the sofa with a book. He loved how she smiled when she saw him. Putting down the book, she sat up as he came to her. Leaning over, he kissed her gently.

"Hi." Last night washed through him, the proposal and her acceptance, and the deep connection he had felt with her when they had made love, so slow and sweet. She melted him with just a touch.

"Hi," she said huskily, and he knew she felt the same.

"I have good news."

"Oooh, I like good news."

"I just met with your father. I paid his loan with Elardi and I'll take over as CEO while we work to save Hadley Forestry."

She smiled big. "Really?" Then her smile dimmed. "What? You met with Elardi?"

"Yes. Yesterday. Took care of the loan this morning."

Her mouth formed an O. "Why didn't you tell me?"

"I didn't want you to worry and I also wanted to surprise you. And now I'm glad I did." She seemed so happy, and he wanted more than anything to *keep* her happy.

"Elardi agreed?"

"I didn't give him much choice." He watched her assimilate why. Trey had probably identified her stalker. The cops were onto Elardi.

"Boy, first you rescue me from that man, and now you've rescued my father." She looped her arms over his shoulders with him still leaning over, one of his hands on the back of the sofa. She kissed him.

"What kind of arrangement did you make with my dad? Did he know you were going to meet with Elardi?"

"No. I didn't tell anyone. He's going to make me CEO."

Her loving look turned to concern. "CEO?"

"Yes, so I have control of the company."

She furrowed her brow. "You want to take control from father?"

"Only as long as it takes to make his company a success."

"You'll report to him, though, right?"

"No. He'll report to me. Temporarily."

She eased away from him and stood. "But…you'll have control, and this is all going to be in writing?"

He hesitated. "Yes."

Now she looked angry. "You're doing exactly what your family did to the Gilfords."

Decker's grandparents had thrown Mara Gilford and Russ Colton together and expanded The Colton Empire—gaining Gilford land. But then the Gilfords, like the Hadleys now, did not have the capital of the Coltons.

"I did it for you, Kendall."

"For *me*?" Her eyes flashed with indignation. "You've stripped him of his life's work. He built Hadley Forestry from nothing."

"He also nearly drove it into the ground."

Kendall turned away, putting her hand to her mouth.

"I thought you'd be happy," Decker said. "Your family's company is going to thrive with me running it."

She pivoted to face him. "Like you don't have enough to do with The Lodge? Maybe you railroaded my father just to ensure you'd be too busy to fall in love with me. Working fourteen, or sixteen hours a day, never home long enough to form any kind of meaningful relationship with me."

Kendall was hurt and more upset than he'd ever seen her.

He stepped toward her. "Darling, I'm sorry. I truly thought this was right for you. I wouldn't be an active executive for long, only as long as it takes to get the company back on track, then I'd hand it back over to your dad."

"But you'd still have controlling interest."

"That is only to ensure I'm allowed to run the company the way I want, without your father interfering."

"It's *his* company, not yours," she snapped.

"His to run into the ground?"

That angered her further, he saw. "My father would do anything to save his company. Why do you think he agreed to your terms? He wouldn't have done that if he didn't feel he had to."

"He made a wise decision," Decker said.

Kendall scoffed and turned her back again, this time storming off. She made it to the entrance of the bedroom before he took her hand and stopped her. He could not let it end like this. She couldn't even look at him, she was so disgusted. Decker had not seen this coming. Could he afford not to have complete control of Hadley Forestry? He felt it would be a huge risk, but looking at Kendall, he also felt cornered to take it.

"Hey." He gently tugged her toward him, until she faced him and was now against him.

She kept her face averted.

Several seconds passed before Decker spoke. "I don't have to have controlling interest if it's going to make you this upset."

Warily she turned to him. She looked so adorable and so sexy, even with her bandage. Her uncovered blue eye sparkled with mistrust. She was such an honest, ethical person. He had to respect that about her.

"I'll invest in the company and be acting CEO only as long as it takes to turn the business around."

Saying nothing, she only continued to look at him. He couldn't tell if she believed him.

"Honestly, Kendall, I did not think you'd be this upset. I'll schedule another meeting with your dad and have new terms drafted."

"You would do that for me?" she asked.

"Of course. You're going to be my wife."

"What if he disagrees with any of your business decisions?" she prodded.

"Then I'll have to convince him why it's the right move to make."

She blinked a few times, mellowing and not appearing so mistrustful. But then she said, "What if you're wrong and he's right?"

"I won't be wrong." He didn't get where he was by being wrong.

Kendall inwardly cheered after her talk with Decker. He may not realize it yet, but he had all the signs of a man falling madly in love. If he didn't have those feelings for her, he wouldn't have altered his business plans for her.

He had surprised her tonight. For such a powerful man he sure did treat her tenderly.

She lay against him on the sofa, watching a movie. He had his legs on the coffee table and his arm around her.

Knocking on the door interrupted them.

She sat up to let him go see who had shown up after dinnertime.

Of course it was his father, Russ. And he didn't look happy.

"I just found out about the deal you made with Bernard." Russ entered.

Decker let the door close as Kendall moved to curl her legs up on the sofa to watch them over the back.

"Who told you?" Decker asked.

"One of the goons you brought with you. Are you planning on turning this family into an enemy of a criminal?"

"No. I diffused a dangerous situation."

He had done that. But what would save Elardi from prosecution if police connected him to the man who'd attempted to kidnap her?

Kendall watched Russ as he took time before he said, "Elardi accepted your terms?"

"Yes."

Russ nodded, seeming satisfied. "And Bernard?"

"He accepted my terms," Decker said, sounding strong and sure.

"Which are?"

"We can talk about this tomorrow. You didn't have to come here this late."

"I'm concerned about you, Decker. What—"

"We already went over this, Dad."

"What terms?" Russ demanded.

Kendall stood and walked over to them. "Decker will be acting CEO until my father's company is back on track. Do you have a problem with that?"

Russ took in her bandaged eye and her defiant stance and then turned back to Decker. "Did you take control of the company?"

"No, but Bernard will let me run it."

Kendall watched Russ simmer with anger, but to his credit he remained calm. And then his anger dissipated as though something else had dawned on him.

"I never thought I'd see the day when a woman would influence your decisions," Russ said.

Decker visibly flinched, though it was so subtle that she doubted Russ even noticed. But *she* had. Kendall had obviously influenced his decision not to take control. What did that mean as far as his feelings for her? She bet he struggled with that right now.

"I'm not saying that's not good," Russ went on. "In

fact, it might motivate you even more." He chuckled, glancing over at Kendall. "My son is falling in love."

Decker's face went still.

Russ gave him a hard pat on his back. "Just make sure you turn a profit on that investment, son."

With another chuckle, Russ headed for the door, opened it and looked back. "See you at the wedding."

Chapter 17

Standing next to Kendall with her in a V-neck, fitted black dress and her hair in a sexy updo, Decker couldn't stop his dad's words from running through his mind, over and over.

My son is falling in love.

He had sounded so definitive. And for his father—the almighty Russ Colton—to say such a thing meant he really believed it. He believed Decker was falling in love.

He was barely aware of the quaint old courthouse where they had gathered with other guests, waiting for Liam and Sloane's wedding to begin. Decker glanced toward the front doors. No sign of the happy couple. The weather had warmed and the sun sparkled in a clear blue sky, a great day for a wedding.

Turning the other way, he looked through the open double doors where wooden seating had been adorned with flowers, brightening the courtroom. He and Kendall would have a church wedding, but this was a unique idea, as well.

Kendall glanced over at him and he met her look, one eye still covered but with a smaller bandage. The blemish didn't matter to him, and her other eye conveyed plenty. That sizzling heat they had, that seemed to have intensified since last night, hit him now. He turned away and caught his older brother Wyatt looking at him, as well as Russ. Decker ignored them.

Although the bride and the groom and little Chloe weren't here yet, Decker and Kendall stood with the rest of the family. Russ and Mara laughed at something Wyatt said, probably joking about Decker falling in love.

Decker had always looked up to his big brother. Tall and wearing his cream Stetson with strands of dark brown hair stuck out from the edge, hints of gray at the temples, he had a rugged look, appropriate for a rancher. He'd always followed his own path.

Bailey Norton, Wyatt's soon-to-be wife, stood beside him, her laugh carrying through the lobby of the courthouse. She moved her long, straight brownish-blond hair back over her shoulder, her dark eyes sparkling.

The twins Skye and Phoebe carried on their own conversation. He sometimes wondered what they shared. They were close, as anyone would expect from twins.

Decker's adopted brother Fox Colton talked with Wyatt and their parents. Decker's younger brother

Blaine was absent. Wyatt and Fox had a lot in common, both ranchers and both loving the outdoors.

A family member of Liam's gave the indication that it was time to enter the courtroom.

Decker let Kendall go ahead and sat on the bride's side. Wyatt sat beside him, his veterinarian fiancée beside him.

"Mom told me about your wedding," Wyatt said. "You sure that's what you want?"

His question ground in his dad's comment deeper. "Yes." Why did he feel a stab of apprehension? He hadn't felt that before. Why did falling in love give him that feeling?

"You're not doing it for Dad, are you?"

Having sat in front of them, Russ and Mara twisted to look back.

"Not anymore he isn't," Russ said. "You saw the way he looks at her."

"Yeah. Hard to miss." Wyatt looked at Bailey and winked.

The two made an attractive couple, but Decker wasn't in the mood to admire that right now. He didn't like being teased about his growing feelings for Kendall.

Kendall had observed the exchange and Decker saw her tiny smile.

"She seems pretty pleased with that, son," Russ said.

He must have noticed her expression, too.

"Go easy on him, Russ," Mara said. "He's never been in love before. This has to be a daunting experience for him."

Wyatt chuckled along with Bailey.

The others quieted and Decker was glad to see Liam enter the courthouse. Sloane waited at the doorway with her daughter Chloe in front of her, holding a basket of flowers. Sloane looked beautiful in a simple white wedding dress. Her dark brown hair had been swept up with a few highlighted tendrils dangling down. She wore a hat with lace. Her daughter wore a matching dress and hat. So adorable.

The magistrate stood in front of his bench, waiting for them, and a harpist began plucking a tune.

In a black suit and tie, Liam reached the magistrate and shook his hand before turning to face Sloane and Chloe.

Sloane bent to talk to little two-year-old Chloe. The girl began walking toward Liam, clumsily sprinkling red flower petals on the floor.

Reaching Liam, she stopped and turned at his guidance toward her mother.

Smiling, Sloane began her walk down the courthouse aisle. When she reached Liam, she took her daughter's hand and they faced the magistrate.

After a brief introductory statement, the magistrate let Liam and Sloane recite the vows they had written for each other and then pronounced them husband and wife. They signed their marriage certificate and faced the small crowd hand in hand.

Decker clapped with everyone else.

Decker's family teasing him had amused Kendall. She sensed a closeness among them, something she wouldn't have expected. The Coltons had such an affluent reputation, and Russ hadn't exactly presented himself as a humble man. But his affection for Decker showed, as did the brotherly love between Wyatt and Decker.

She stood beside Decker at the wedding reception, held at Russ and Mara's mansion in the lower-level rec room. Country music played in the background.

Decker was in the midst of chatting with the groom while Bailey and Wyatt had begun an intimate game of pool. Russ and Mara talked business, sitting on the sectional before a giant screen that was currently dark. Skye and Fox played a game of darts as though this were another casual family gathering and Phoebe sat on a tall stool watching them.

"How is your eye?" Sloane asked Kendall.

Kendall looked at Sloane's pretty heart-shaped face "Oh, it's fine. I have cosmetic surgery scheduled. The doctors are confident the scarring will be minimal to nonexistent."

"What a relief. Who would do such a thing?" Sloane asked. "I know Trey said it could be racially motivated, but still."

"Yeah. Some people are so scary." Kendall looked at Decker, thinking of her stalker and thankful she had him to help keep her safe.

"My former in-laws tried to off me, so believe me, I know," Sloane said. "Liam saved me." She sent her new husband a warm smile.

He returned it and slipped his arm around her, light

green eyes sparkling in his youthful face. "It was nothing."

The conversation fell into a lull while Liam and Sloane shared a silent exchange of love with only their eyes. Kendall saw Wyatt and Bailey behaving similarly and admired them for a while. Wyatt was tall and ruggedly handsome and Bailey slender and sexy, something Wyatt clearly noticed with the way he looked at her and the way his hand occasionally touched her as they moved around the pool table to take shots.

"What's going on with the Rouge murder case?" Decker asked Liam.

"Still no new leads."

"Do you think Bianca was kidnapped before she was killed and left at Wyatt's ranch?" Kendall asked.

"We're not ruling it out."

There was so much going on in Roaring Springs, unusual things. The town was normally a quiet getaway and now a woman had been murdered and another disappeared. For a moment, Kendall wondered if her stalker could be involved in either, but quickly dismissed that, since Emilio Elardi most likely had hired the man.

"You still concerned about a decline in reservations?" Liam asked.

"I haven't seen a notable improvement." He glanced at Kendall. "We've set up a charity event for next month. Advertising for that seems to be generating a lot of interest, so maybe in the next few weeks we'll see some more traffic. It's good PR and good to support a cause as worthy as helping victims of sex trafficking."

Chloe tugged on her mother's dress. "I have to go."

"Bathroom time." Sloane took Chloe's hand and walked away. Fox came over and started talking to Liam. Those two wandered over to the bar, leaving Kendall alone with Decker.

Kendall resumed watching Wyatt and Bailey and in her peripheral vision saw Decker follow where she looked.

"How did they meet?" she asked.

"Wyatt was a bull rider in the rodeo and Bailey was a barrel racer. That was before she went to college to become a veterinarian."

"A barrel racer?" She looked at him. "They've been together that long? I thought—"

"No," he interrupted. "They were married a long time ago and just got back together. Bailey had some issues with her past and needed some time to sort that out. At least, that's what Wyatt told me."

What did she have to sort out? From the looks of them, they should have never parted ways.

"Do we look like that together?" she asked.

He turned his head sharply toward her. Maybe she was pushing him too much. He'd already endured his family's poking.

"They're so in love," she added.

"I don't know. *Do* we look like that together?" he asked, throwing the ball back in her court.

She thought of all the times she felt all warm and tingly with him. "Yes, but I don't think anyone has seen us like that."

"According to my family, they have." He sounded annoyed.

She laughed lightly and faced him, sliding her hands onto his chest. "Don't worry. There are worse things that can happen to you than falling in love."

The set of his mouth and eyes told her he wasn't happy to hear that. "Wyatt and Bailey like each other."

"No." She jabbed her thumb in the other couple's direction. "*That* is *love*."

He put his hands on her waist.

"Why do you fight it so much?" she asked softly.

"I'm not."

"So you truly believe you aren't falling in love?"

"I'm beginning to doubt that," he finally admitted.

Kendall was sure his father had the most influence on his change of heart. Decker hadn't admitted he *was* falling for her, but she'd take the next best thing.

She smiled up at him but her joy dimmed when she noticed that Mara and Russ's conversation had turned heated. Decker stepped back from Kendall and faced them along with everyone else in the room. Mara was clearly upset about something.

"Why didn't you tell me?" she demanded of her husband.

Russ appeared contrite. "I'm sorry. He asked me not to say anything."

"And you thought that included me? I'm his *mother*. I have every bit as much right to know what he tells you as you do."

"Mara—"

Mara stood. "Don't Mara me. Go away!"

Russ stood. "Sweetheart, I'm sorry."

Decker walked over to them. "Give us a minute, Dad."

Russ looked from his wife to Decker.

"Give her some space for a little while," Decker said.

Russ grumbled something and then left the room.

"Mom, what happened?" Decker asked.

"Blaine called him." Her voice trembled she was so upset. "He told Russ he's back in the States."

Decker's youngest brother had joined the army and none of them had seen him in almost two years.

"He called Russ but not me," Mara complained, obviously injured that her son had chosen Russ over her. "He wouldn't tell Russ where he had been all this time, only that he was part of Special Forces."

"Maybe he can't talk about what he does, Mom," Decker soothed. "If he's in Special Forces, his missions might be classified."

"I know, but he could have called his own mother to let her know he was all right and he would be coming home soon."

Kendall wouldn't argue that. If she had a son in the military, she'd worry every minute of the day if he was all right.

"Knowing Blaine, he didn't mean to upset you. He called Dad because you would have pried information out of him that he isn't at liberty to share. You're his mother. He loves you. You have to know that."

Mara began to calm. "Russ should have told me he called."

"Yes, he should have," Decker agreed.

"I'm not speaking to him for a long time."

Decker chuckled and brought his mother in for a brief hug. "You'll get over it. Dad didn't mean to hurt you, either."

"Sometimes I wonder."

Russ's first love would always be his company, but when it came to their kids, he should have known better than to keep a secret like that from Mara.

After a delightful evening that had improved after Mara forgave Russ about an hour later, Decker held the front door of the mansion open for Kendall and they stepped out into the night. The temperature had cooled considerably

After helping Kendall into the passenger side, Decker got behind the wheel and drove away from the mansion. He merged onto the dark highway and kept to the speed limit, but he couldn't wait to get back to The Lodge so he could be alone with his beautiful fiancée. She leaned back against the seat of the McLaren, looking content and a little sleepy. He was beginning to recognize her moods and he adored every one of them. He would do anything for her, he realized. Anything to make her happy. He was happy if she was happy.

Was that love?

If he never knew with absolute certainty, how would he *ever* know? He always came back to the same dilemma. When he had admitted his growing doubt that his original conviction might be wrong, he saw how much that had meant to Kendall and probably explained her contentment.

A loud bang erupted followed by another and Decker lost control of the car. It felt like two of his tires had just blown out. Kendall let out a startled shriek as the car swerved off the road. The tires caught on something just before he drove over a rock that the low-framed McLaren couldn't clear.

The bump jolted him and Kendall and Decker couldn't bring the car back onto the highway. It ran into a tree.

Seconds later, he shook off his faint disorientation and quickly checked on Kendall. She put her hand to her head near her bandage.

"Are you okay?" He unfastened his seat belt and leaned over to her.

"My head hit the window," she said. "What happened?"

"That's what I'm about to find out." Decker couldn't tell if her head had broken the glass or the impact had. The passenger door had bent and now hung open to the cooling air. He unfastened her seat belt, worried what had caused his tires to blow. He searched around and didn't see anyone. The bangs had sounded like gunshots.

He took out his phone and called Trey. As he did that, he spotted a shadow in the rearview mirror, which was still aligned on the cracked windshield.

"Decker? Everything all right?" he heard Trey say.

"He's attacking us on the highway!" He got out of the car as a man ran to Kendall's side. Decker sprinted around the car, but not before the guy dragged Kendall out of it. She struggled and the fellow was about to point a gun to her head.

"You had to go and meddle, didn't you," the attacker hissed. "It's because of you that I can't go home. I can't go anywhere! You deserve to die for that."

"We're on the highway on the way to The Lodge!" Decker shouted and then threw his phone with Trey still talking, hitting the man in the eye. Kendall got away, running to Decker and then behind the McLaren.

Reaching the stranger as he began to bring the pistol around, Decker knocked his hand hard and blocked the other from swinging to hit him. He had a clear view of his face. He had dark hair and eyes and an acne-scarred face. He was shorter than Decker by only a half inch or so.

"No way you live!" the man roared. "Both of you are going to die!"

Decker grabbed the guy's wrist and slammed it down on the edge of the bent door.

The man hollered in pain and the gun fell into the McLaren.

Decker slammed a punch into the attacker's stomach. He had to maintain the upper hand. This man was a trained killer.

He kicked the guy as he was hunched over, knocking him to the ground. Then Decker bent inside the McLaren for the gun. Retrieving that, he felt the man hook an arm around his neck and begin to choke him.

Then suddenly the man eased away and fell down.

Decker turned with the gun and saw Kendall had picked up a rock she had used to hit the man on the head.

Decker pointed the gun at the fallen man, who blinked up at him, dazed.

Kendall dropped the rock and rushed to him. He put his arm around her.

He heard sirens. Finally it was over.

Moments later, Daria arrived with several other officers and then Trey showed up shortly after. He must have made an emergency call.

Daria took the dark-haired man away in handcuffs as Trey jogged over to them.

"Are you both all right?"

"Yes. We're okay," Kendall said.

Decker was immensely relieved to hear her say that, but asked anyway, "Are you sure?"

"Yes."

"Good. The timing for this is impeccable. I just got off the phone with an officer in the county where Emilio's casino is. They made an arrest. Just this afternoon, a witness came forward and identified him as the man who paid to have someone kidnapped and then he saw him kill the victim."

"Who came forward?"

"One of his henchmen. Apparently he learned of the attempt to kidnap Kendall and that police have identified the would-be kidnapper. He was afraid to go forward before, but not anymore."

Kendall sagged against Decker with a sigh.

"Oh, that's great news," she said.

"The witness will get some time for his crimes but it won't be nearly as stiff and what Emilio is facing," Trey said. "He's going to be in jail for a long time."

Now they wouldn't have to look over their shoulders, always wondering if Emilio would decide to take revenge.

Decker felt like celebrating. He glanced over at his prized sports car.

"Looks like you'll have to get another car," Kendall said.

"I'll have someone call for a tow," Trey told them. "Were you insured?"

Decker grunted a laugh. "It wouldn't pay to insure a car like this."

"Come on, I'll give you a lift back to The Lodge," he said.

Decker was all for that, although his earlier anticipation of being alone with Kendall had changed from wanting a romantic night to just having a peaceful one.

Chapter 18

The next morning, Kendall woke to the sound of wind rumbling against the lodge walls. She opened her eyes to Decker's head resting inches from hers. She took in his handsome, sleeping face for a while and then got up to look out the window. The sun had risen long ago but she could only see about twenty feet from the lodge. Then it was a complete whiteout.

She lay back down. Decker's eyes fluttered open and he met hers.

A slow, lazy smile crept up. "Good morning, beautiful."

The sound of his gruff voice still heavy with sleep and yet full of tenderness gave her now-familiar tingles.

"Good morning."

"Looks like it's going to be a stay-in-bed day," he said.

"Mmm. That would be delightful. Find us a movie."

"Do you want breakfast or lunch to start with?" He propped pillows up and lifted the phone next to the bed.

"Brunch." They hadn't eaten much for dinner. She was hungry. "Fruit."

"Prime rib?" He handed her the remote control for the television.

She took it and pressed the power button. "And eggs."

"Henry's makes a great avocado egg toast." He pressed for room service. "This is Decker. I'd like to order brunch." He rattled off a list of items that made her mouth water.

When he finished, he leaned back against the headboard while she searched out a movie, settling on a romantic comedy. Propping her pillows, she reclined next to him. About thirty minutes into the movie, someone knocked on the door.

Decker got up, slipped on a pair of jeans and went to let room service in. A young man in a white shirt with a black vest and pants pushed a table inside. Decker directed him into the bedroom and the man set up the table, complete with a white linen tablecloth and a vase of carnations. In her nightgown, she had covers up to her chest, feeling just a little awkward with the stranger in the room. She was sure he'd seen a lot delivering room service, though.

Decker tipped him and the man left.

After taking off his jeans, Decker removed the plate covers and climbed back onto the bed. While they watched the movie, he fed her breakfast, starting with strawberries and sips of champagne with orange juice.

He seemed very involved in the task, letting his fingers touch her lips as he fed her strawberries, and looking deeply into her eyes. The avocado-and-egg toast was delicious.

As he reached for another bite, she stopped him. "Wait. It's your turn." Pushing covers aside, she straddled him and picked up his toast, first taking a bite and then putting it to his mouth. He took a bite and egg yolk oozed out the corner of his mouth.

Unable to resist, she leaned over and kissed him, removing the yolk. As passion intensified, he sank his fingers into her hair and kissed her harder.

Kendall drew back, absorbing his smoldering face. She picked up a glass of champagne and orange juice and took a sip, feeling sultry. Then she gave him a sip.

Setting that aside, no longer hungry for food, she caressed his face. She ran her thumbs over lips she so loved kissing, over his cheekbones and then trailed her forefinger over his brow. Holding his face between her hands, she kissed him reverently, wishing for him to feel the strength of her love.

He tugged at her nightgown and she rose up to allow him to lift it over her head. Now only in underwear, she moved herself against his hardness. Flattening her hands on his chest, she leaned over to kiss him again, gliding over his lips and feeling him move with her.

His hands ran down her back, giving her a shiver. He cupped his hands on her rear and pressed her against him, grinding slowly.

Kendall let out a held breath with the incredible sensation that caused. She kissed him again and again, not getting enough of him.

"You make me feel so good," he murmured.

"You make me feel like I'm going out of my mind." She kissed him. "If this isn't love, I don't know what is."

The last came out almost of its own accord. She hadn't meant to say that aloud. But now that she had, she felt him stiffen.

He looked up at her with a hint of confusion, not fully able to hide it from her, as she was sure he tried to do. To distract him, she came down for more soft, heartfelt kisses. After a few more of those, she traced her tongue along his lips, top then bottom, and then found her way inside when he parted them, responding to her passion with his own.

She hooked her fingers on the hem of his underwear and pulled down. He lifted his hips and she shoved them all the way down, using her toes. Then she rose up onto her knees, moving them close together and looking at Decker as she slid her panties down.

He watched.

On her hands and knees, she kicked her underwear off and then straddled him again. Sitting on him, she ran her hands up his chest and back down, loving the feel of his hard muscles and his ridged abdomen. Keeping her hands there, she rubbed herself on his length.

His gruff breaths came with his hands on her hips. He lifted her and she guided his member to her opening.

Kendall moaned as she lowered onto him. She tingled everywhere. A shudder rippled through her. She had to go still or she'd detonate.

Decker had other ideas. He began to raise and lower his hips. She rocked on him. His thrusts grew harder and faster.

Kendall couldn't control the escalating sensations. She tipped her head back and came hard, unable to stop the guttural, "Ah," from erupting.

He made a sound too. As the firestorm calmed, she kept moving on him. She could have another orgasm. She rocked and ground herself, coherent enough to look into his eyes as another climax rose. The sensation rolled through her, gripped her and then released her from heavenly tortuous bliss.

Collapsing on him, she eased to his side with little aftershocks racking her. This was the most intense it had been between them. Was it possible to die of extreme pleasure?

Decker stroked her hair and she rested her hand on his chest. She needed some time to float back down to earth.

After a few minutes, she moved so she could see him. He met her eyes, looking sated and relaxed.

"How was it for you?" she asked.

He grinned. "You have to ask?"

"It was life-altering for me."

He didn't say anything and she left him to his thoughts. Getting more comfortable beside him, she watched the movie for a while.

"Have you ever had sex like that with anyone else?" he asked.

"No." She looked at him. "Not even close."

He seemed disturbed over something. Kendall didn't have to guess what that was.

"Have you ever *felt* this way for anyone else?" he asked.

He obviously needed to know in order to understand his own feelings. "No." Not by a long shot. There was absolutely no comparison. "Have you?"

After a lengthy pause, he said in a quiet tone, "No."

Kendall didn't push him or say what came to mind just then. *Then this had to be love. True love.*

Kendall fell asleep beside him as they watched the movie. He was too plagued by the earth-shattering sex he'd just experienced. It had been the same for her. Neither of them had ever felt like this with anyone else. That had to mean something.

If this isn't love, I don't know what is.

Kendall's words haunted him—or more like *taunted* him. For so long he'd been convinced love was a rarity that would never happen to him. He even doubted whether anyone really felt that kind of pure love. Life wasn't all roses and cheer. Life was difficult. Life had to be *survived*. And humans weren't even-tempered creatures. Moods and personalities complicated relationships. Wouldn't fairy-tale kind of love be void of that? He had thought the only way for that kind of love to be real was if two people got along so well that they never fought and always agreed on everything.

The fact was, Decker was the kind of man who had to have proof that something was real or believable. He had no proof that what he and Kendall had was true love. He would never have proof.

Turning his head, he watched her sleep, her blond hair a mess and face soft and quiet, the bandage still covering her right eye. Her left hand rested on his chest, the diamond ring he'd given her sparkling.

How could he know what he felt for her? What kind of test could he put on himself?

Could he live without her?

As his thoughts wandered over the last nearly four weeks, he had his answer. He would be unhappy without her. She enriched his life. He felt joy when he was with her.

He wanted to spend the rest of his life with her, and not because he thought she'd make him a good wife and a good mother to his children. He wanted to spend the rest of his life *with her*.

Kendall's eyes opened just then. She saw him watching her and a soft smile emerged.

"I love you," he murmured. As he said the words, he believed them.

Her smile remained and she didn't appear surprised. "I know. I'm glad you finally admitted it."

He leaned down and kissed her. He wouldn't have believed he could feel any stronger for her, but he did. Kissing her held so much more meaning now.

He kissed her until they were both feverish for each other, then he rolled on top of her. She parted her legs and he moved between them, not stopping his kisses as he sank into her.

"Decker. Oh," she uttered breathlessly.

"I know," he answered her. "I feel it too." e thrust into her.

She put her hands up against the headboard and cried, "Yes! Harder, Decker."

The heat of their joining spiraled out of control. He slammed into her, needed to satisfy this intense love. If that was even possible.

She came and so did he. It was over in a matter of minutes.

Lowering down onto her, he caught his breath with her, loving the warmth and the sound. Most of all he loved being this close to this beautiful, enchanting woman, feeling as though they were one.

Chapter 19

Kendall stood before the full-length mirror in the church room they'd given her to prepare for the wedding. The dress was every bit as beautiful as the day she'd first seen it.

Silver-white reflective beads of varying sizes and shapes and round white pearls decorated the bodice, which dipped low enough to provide some cleavage. The pearls ran down each rib of the corset and the beads thinned over the see-through lace stomach. More beadwork at the waist dipped to a V at the lower abdomen. She turned to admire the back; the Cinderella-style skirt had no train, just a puff of tulle.

Her mother came to stand beside her. "You look beautiful."

Kendall smiled.

"But you're missing one thing."

Kendall eyed her mother and then watched her lift a strand of pearls. "These belonged to your great-great grandmother." She hung the necklace around Kendall's neck. "She gave it to her daughter on her wedding day, your great-grandmother. And then your great grandmother gave it to my mother, who gave it to me on my wedding day."

Fingering the old pearls, Kendall gaped at her mother. "You never told me about that."

"It never came up. I always knew I'd give them to you on your wedding day. I've kept them stored away all these years. They're probably worth around ten thousand by now. Your great-great grandmother received them from her husband on their first wedding anniversary in eighteen seventy-four."

"Wow. They're lovely." Kendall looked in the mirror and saw the elaborate platinum clasp with sapphires and diamonds.

"I was reminded of them when you bought this dress and I could barely keep them a secret from you. I knew they'd be perfect."

Kendall turned and hugged her mother. "Thank you, Mom."

Her mom hugged her back. "I love you, honey. I hope you're happy from this day on to your last with that incredible man who's waiting out there for you. I've been happy with your father for the most part—up until he started losing his mind in business deals."

Kendall laughed, hearing her mother's dry sense of humor.

"It's time." Kendall turned with her mother to see her father in the doorway.

"I'll go take my seat." Marion kissed Kendall's cheek and left the room.

Going out into the hall with her dad, she hooked her arm with his.

"Ready?" he asked.

"Yes." Kendall truly did feel ready for this—marrying Decker.

She walked with her dad to the auditorium. The church dated back to the 1850s and was originally a wood structure. It was renovated in the late 1800s and built of stone. The original terrazzo floor, gold leaf and stained glass windows had been meticulously restored.

Her breath caught as she continued to bask in all the surrounding splendor. The round stone-framed windows were high up and predominantly blue, with orange, red, green and yellow mixed in the pattern. She recalled Skye telling her that the sanctuary had Breccia Violetta marble columns that had been brought in from Italy. Her gaze then drifted to the pews which had cream-colored flowers at the ends and more large bouquets decorated the altar.

The little church was full of people, some she recognized, others she didn't. They all stood and someone began playing a traditional wedding march tune on a piano.

Kendall walked with her father down the aisle. Decker stood with the pastor at the altar, hands folded in front of him, looking tall and big and handsome in his black tuxedo. Everything else fell away except for him. This felt so right.

"Who gives this woman to wed this man?" the pastor asked.

"I do," Bernard answered.

Her father handed her over to Decker. She placed her hand in his and stepped up onto the altar beside him.

The piano music stopped and the pastor began the ceremony, welcoming the guests to their nuptials.

"We are gathered here today to unite Decker and Kendall in a pledge of love and best wishes for a lifetime of happiness together," the pastor said. "This joining of two families will be marked on this very special day as we witness their commitment, a commitment that would not have taken place had these two souls not crossed paths on their journey through life up to this point in time.

"Many of you may have been surprised to hear of this wedding announcement. Decker and Kendall have not been together long, only a month. But Decker asked me to point out that these two have known each other most of their lives. They went to the same school, and although they didn't spend any time getting to know each other better, they were each aware of the other's existence." The pastor addressed her and Decker. "It turns out the two of you are perfect together."

Kendall smiled at Decker, who smiled back along with a few admiring murmurs from the crowd.

"And so it is, Decker and Kendall join together today, surrounded by the people closest to them," the pastor continued. "If there be anyone who has cause why this couple should not be united in marriage, they must speak now or forever hold their peace."

The pastor paused.

"I do."

Kendall turned with Decker to see Russ grinning.

"I'm kidding."

A few people chuckled. Kendall shared a mockingly skeptical glance with Decker before facing the pastor again.

"We can't claim that divine influence brought these two souls together. This began as an arranged marriage, but something happened in just one month's time. Kendall's memory of Decker from high school brought her to their first dinner. In kind, Decker's memory of Kendall made him indulge his father's wishes and he too agreed to that first dinner."

"Love doesn't come easy to most of us," the pastor said. "We love our family. We love our friends. But love between a man and a woman is something no one can predict. It begins with emotional love and grows into special companionship. Trust is the most important ingredient to love. Without trust, you have no respect. Without trust, you have no freedom to offer your whole heart to another person."

The pastor again addressed only the bride and the groom. "Love and only love brought you here today. As your lives go forth from this day, never forget what brought you here. Never forget that it is love that will make your marriage last because you both came here freely, of your own will, in the name of love."

The pastor looked across the crowd. "Now I'd like

to share a reading from Corinthians 13:1-3 titled 'Love Is Indispensable.' Though I speak with the tongues of men and of angels, and have not charity, I am become as sounding brass, or a tinkling cymbal. And though I have the gift of prophecy, and understand all mysteries, and all knowledge, and though I have all faith, so that I could remove mountains, and have not charity, I am nothing. And though I bestow all my goods to feed the poor, and though I give my body to be burned, and have not charity, it profiteth me nothing.

"Love," the pastor said, "is the key to all success and happiness." Then he looked at Kendall and Decker. "Please face each other and join hands."

Kendall faced Decker and put her hands in his.

"Kendall, do you freely and without hesitation give yourself to Decker in marriage? Do you promise to love, honor, cherish and protect him, forsaking all others and holding only to him forevermore?"

"I do," she said.

"And Decker, do you freely and without hesitation give yourself to Kendall in marriage? Do you promise to love, honor, cherish and protect her, forsaking all others and holding only to her forevermore?

"I do." Decker's deep voice resounded in the auditorium.

"Do you have rings?"

Decker removed Kendall's ring from his pocket and she untied his from a ribbon around her bouquet.

"Decker and Kendall have written their own vows. Decker, will you begin?"

Decker held the ring at the tip of her finger. "I ask

you to accept this ring as a reminder that it was you who taught me love. You showed me love. From this day forward, I promise to be faithful to you, to respect you and to forever be grateful that you're in my life."

Kendall had to fight the sting of joyful tears. He hadn't shared his vows with her. She hadn't shared hers, either. They'd only agreed to begin with "I ask you to accept this ring" and to make one promise to each other.

He slipped the ring on her finger.

Kendall held his ring at the tip of his finger. "I ask you to accept this ring as a symbol of my love for you. I didn't plan on falling in love, but you showed me I could trust you with my heart and soul. I promise to always be your best friend and lover and to be by your side for all the days of my life."

"By the power vested in me, I now pronounce you husband and wife," the pastor said, smiling fondly, then to Decker he said, "You may kiss the bride."

Decker moved close and kissed her softly. The guests clapped and some cheered.

"I now present to you, Mr. and Mrs. Colton." The pastor went on to announce the reception, which would be held at The Chateau.

Decker never imagined he'd be married *and* in love—and now he felt like the luckiest man alive. For food they'd opted for hors d'oeuvres. After cutting the cake, taking pictures and their first dance, he and Kendall had dispersed to mingle among family and friends. He couldn't stop looking at her, though, and noticed her doing the same with him.

"You're going to set the floor on fire."

Turning, he saw Skye standing beside him.

"It's really good to see you so happy," she said. "I was worried about you."

"You should have more faith in me."

Skye looked at Kendall, who glanced at Decker again.

"She's really a great woman," Skye said. "We all like her."

"I'm glad you approve."

"Even Dad does now."

He rolled his eyes. "Only because he thinks I'll be motivated to turn Hadley Forestry into a profitable company again."

"Of course. The Colton Empire is his firstborn baby."

Decker watched Kendall dance with her father and Russ dance with Mara. Wyatt and Bailey did a bouncy two-step, Wyatt twirling her with surprising finesse.

Phoebe showed up on his other side. "Skye and I had a lot of fun setting this up."

"Yeah, turned out pretty nice."

It was nice, very upscale. The hors d'oeuvres had been created by an expert chef who had made them look like art.

"Dad told me there's a big developer here who isn't happy with his lumber supplier," Sloane said, pointing across the room. "His name is Nicolas Stone. Dad invited him to the wedding so you could talk to him."

Decker grunted derisively. "Always working." Decker walked across the room and headed for Nicolas Stone.

The man saw him coming. About six feet tall and slightly on the heavy side, he was around sixty and had graying dark hair.

"Decker Colton?" Stone said.

Decker shook his hand. "Yes. Thanks for coming."

"Congratulations."

"Thanks."

"You father invited me so I could have a word with you. I told him it could wait but he insisted."

Decker nodded. "That sounds like my dad. How can I help you?"

"I run the Colorado division for Stone Homes."

Decker had heard of it—a large developer with a presence all over the country.

"I've been getting my lumber from another supplier. Actually, I was going to reach out to Hadley Forestry to see if we can work a deal."

"I'd love to. I'm sure we can arrange something both of us will like."

"I already like the beetle kill harvesting," Stone said. "That's why I wanted to call you. Then I ran into Russ and he told me you were acting as CEO for the company."

"I am."

"Good. Let's set up a meeting after your honeymoon." Mr. Stone took out a business card.

Decker took it.

"Now go enjoy the rest of your wedding reception."

Decker couldn't believe his luck. Today was indeed a very special day. He thanked the man and walked over to Kendall, who sat with her mother and Sloane at a table.

He extended his hand. "I'd like to spend some time with my wife."

She put her hand in his and stood. "I'd like to spend some time with my husband."

A slow song had started. Wyatt and Bailey were still on the dance floor. Decker escorted Kendall there, seeing Liam take Sloane's hand and follow.

"Who was that man you were talking to?" Kendall asked.

"Our new client. Stone Homes is in the market for a new lumber supplier. We're going to meet in the next week or two to talk terms."

Her smile had widened and her mouth dropped open. "That's great news!"

He slow-danced her in a circle.

"You must be my lucky charm," she said.

"Looks like I won't have to act as CEO after all, at least, not for long. I was thinking about spending less time at The Lodge and more time at home with you. Maybe set some regular hours so I'm home at a decent hour every night. How does that sound?"

"Not like Decker Colton." She laughed. "But it sounds great to me."

"There will be nights that run long, but for the most part I bet we can make it work."

"You can make anything work." She kissed him as they moved in each other's arms. "Oh, I talked with your dad earlier. He said there are some avalanche warnings across the state. The way the weather has been around here, you might want to keep an eye on the mountain."

"Yeah, we talked about that too. I've already put a watch in effect."

The weather had gone from warm to cold and they'd had that big storm. Colorado could be dangerous in the spring. Another big spring storm was forecast for tomorrow. The Wicked slope was steep enough to be prone to avalanches, and often had to be cleared.

"That's my man, always prepared and proactive." She looped her arms over his shoulders.

Decker enjoyed her happy eyes and kissed her again.

"Keep that up and we're going to have to leave early."

"When you put it that way…" He kissed her again, this time lingering.

"Decker…"

"We might as well get started on a family," he murmured.

"No need to rush anything. I want to enjoy you for a while."

He held her close against him as they danced in a circle.

"Hey, you have a room at The Lodge," Wyatt quipped as he and Bailey danced next to them.

"You're one to talk," Decker answered.

Wyatt chuckled and swung his woman around as the song changed to something more upbeat.

"When do you want to start a family?" he asked when his brother was no longer within earshot. "That's one thing we didn't really talk about." There was a lot they hadn't talked about, only having been together romantically for one month.

"Maybe in a year. You okay with that?"

"Darling, I am fine with whatever makes you happy."

She beamed up at him. "For such a powerful man you sure are nice to me."

"Nice?" He stopped dancing. "About leaving early…"

She looked around as though searching for a way to sneak out.

"I know a way." He took her hand and headed for the back doors that led to the kitchen area. He'd never felt more alive than he did now and sensed Kendall sharing that sentiment. He was going to love his new life. With her.

* * * * *

Don't miss the previous volumes in the Coltons of Roaring Springs *miniseries:*

Colton Cowboy Standoff *by Marie Ferrarella*
Colton Under Fire *by Cindy Dees*

Available now from
Harlequin Romantic Suspense.

And don't miss the next Coltons book,
Colton's Secret Bodyguard *by Jane Godman,*
Coming in April 2019!

COMING NEXT MONTH FROM

H HARLEQUIN®

ROMANTIC suspense

Available April 2, 2019

#2035 COLTON'S SECRET BODYGUARD
The Coltons of Roaring Springs
by Jane Godman
When Bree Colton receives threats against her life, her parents immediately hire Rylan Bennet to be her secret bodyguard. As the threats to Bree move to attacks, the pair grows closer, but Rylan's secret identity may prove to be too much for Bree.

#2036 OPERATION HERO'S WATCH
Cutter's Code
by Justine Davis
Jace Cahill never expected to have to keep his promise to look out for his best friend's little sister. But now Cassie Grant has a stalker and only Jace—with the help of Cutter and the Foxworth Foundation—can help her.

#2037 TEXAS RANCH JUSTICE
by Karen Whiddon
When Scarlett Kistler travels to Texas to meet the father she never knew, she faces a hostile but handsome ranch foreman, Travis Warren, and her father's mysterious illness. Can the burgeoning love between Travis and Scarlett survive in the face of intrigue and attempted murder?

#2038 RANGER'S BABY RESCUE
Rangers of Big Bend
by Lara Lacombe
When Emma Foster's baby is kidnapped by her brother, she suspects he's taken the little girl to Big Bend National Park. When she enlists the help of park ranger Matthew Thompson, however, they discover a much larger plot is afoot.

HRSCNM0319

Scarlett's voice broke and she looked down, valiantly
struggling to regain emotional control.

Travis could no more have remained in his chair than he
could have stopped breathing. He took a few steps and dropped
down beside her, then gathered her in his arms and held her.

Like before, his body instantly responded to her softness.
And like before, he kept his desire under control. "I'm sorry,"
he murmured, allowing himself the pleasure of caressing her
back and shoulders. "I can only imagine how much that hurts."

"And now I'm facing losing Hal before I even get to know
him," she continued. "Worse, we have no idea what we're
battling, so it's difficult to get together a cohesive defense."

He managed something that he hoped sounded like assent.
She wiggled slightly, nestling closer to him. Desire zinged
through his veins, and he had to shift his body so she wouldn't
recognize his growing arousal.

How could this tiny woman make him desire her without
even trying?

"Travis?" She tilted her face to look up at him, her lips parted. "Would you do me a favor?"

At that moment, he would have promised her the moon. "I'll try," he answered. "What is it?"

"Would you kiss me again?" she breathed.

Just like that, she managed to rip away every shred of the armor he'd attempted to build around him. With a groan, he lowered his mouth to her, claiming her lips with a hunger that tore through and gutted him.

Rock hard, he could barely move, never mind think. While he wasn't entirely sure she knew what she was doing to him, he knew if she kept it up, he'd lose the last shred of what little self-control he'd managed to hang on to.

"Scarlett," he growled.

She must have heard the warning in his voice, because her hands stilled. Though she didn't move away from him, not yet. And she had to, because right now the only movement he felt capable of making would be ripping off their clothes and pushing himself up inside of her.

"We need to stop," he made himself say.

"Do we?" Pushing slightly back, she gazed up at him, her lips swollen from his kisses and her eyes dark with desire.

Don't miss
Texas Ranch Justice *by Karen Whiddon,*
available April 2019 wherever
Harlequin® Romantic Suspense books
and ebooks are sold.

www.Harlequin.com

ROMANTIC suspense

Heart-racing romance, breathless suspense

Don't miss Justine Davis's new Cutter's Code thriller!

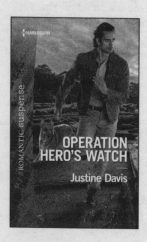

*Reunited in peril...
and united in love?*

When a stalker haunts Cassidy Grant's every move, she turns to Jace Cahill to keep her safe. Pretty soon Jace realizes that his best friend's little sister is all grown up. But with danger menacing, can the brilliant guard dog Cutter keep Cassidy safe...and nudge her and Jace toward the scariest proposition of all—a future together?

Available April 2019